mrs
jekyll

emma glass

CHEERIO

First published in Great Britain in 2024 by
CHEERIO Publishing
www.cheeriopublishing.com
info@cheeriopublishing.com

Cover design: Mark and Keith at Mini Moderns®
Book design: Tiana-Jane Dunlop
Printed and bound in Great Britain by TJ Books Limited.

Cover photograph: 'And For This Sin There Is No Remedy' (2023),
by Juno Calypso
Reproduced by kind permission of Juno Calypso

The moral right of the author has been asserted.

A CIP catalogue record for this book is available from the British Library.

ISBN: 978-1-7394405-6-5
eISBN: 978-1-917283-00-7

Emma Glass's debut novel *Peach* was published by Bloomsbury in 2018 and was longlisted for the International Dylan Thomas Prize. Her second novel, *Rest and Be Thankful*, was published in 2020. Born in Wales, Glass is based in London where she works as children's nurse.

'*Mrs Jekyll* is a raw and affecting novel ... There's anger here, and pain, but also humour, wit, and a joyful letting go.'
- Clare Fisher, author of *All The Good Things*

'*Mrs Jekyll* is a bruising exploration of agency and loss. Incisive and mercurial, Emma Glass takes the classic Jekyll and Hyde story and makes it entirely her own. A searing, feminist account of how it feels to be at war with yourself, and the desire to live and die in a world that can no longer contain you.'
- Jessica Andrews, author of *Saltwater* and *Milk Teeth*

'*Mrs Jekyll* is a gripping re-imagining of the classic gothic tale. Glass's writing is daringly sensuous, intoxicating, compelling the reader towards a devastating finale.'
- Naomi Booth, author of *Sealed*

'Sensual, chilling, powerfully immersive, Emma Glass writes with a truly original voice.'
- Esther Freud, author of *Hideous Kinky* and *I Couldn't Love You More*

'An elegant, intricately crafted book which takes the classic story into a whole new dimension, *Mrs Jekyll* captured my attention from the very first page. We meet Rosy Winter, a protagonist so engaging that her observations of her illness, womanhood and the world are powerfully visceral and cut close to the bone – a true gift for readers everywhere. Emma Glass has created a piece of such exquisite work that it will enthrall a whole generation of readers. A huge win for literature, the elemental and potent *Mrs Jekyll* is one of my favourite books this year.'
- Nikita Gill, author of *Wild Embers*

'*Mrs Jekyll* ripped through me: all the softness and terror is bound together by precise lyrical prose and Glass's extraordinary attention for detail. Read once in a gulp and a second time for the beauty.'
- Sarvat Hasin, author of *You Can't Go Home Again* and *The Giant Dark*

'Glass makes us look in the uncomfortable places, to see the things we want to turn away from. The result, *Mrs Jekyll*, is fiction that feels truer than biography.'
- Rowan Hisayo Buchanan, author of *Harmless Like You*, *Starling Days* and *The Sleep Watcher*

'*Mrs Jekyll* is a heartbreaking and seductive novel – a swirling journey into grief's abandon that is both dark and beautifully-wrought.'
- Sophie Mackintosh, author of *The Water Cure*

'Emma Glass is one of the most distinctive and exciting literary novelists around, with a poet's heart and a surgical sensibility about what is unsettling, puzzling and sublime about the world. *Mrs Jekyll* takes a well-known premise and elevates it to something searing and vividly contemporary, I have never seen a depiction of the deterioration of desire between a young couple, caused by illness and physical decline, in quite this way. I read the novel in one sitting, and I found it moving and disturbing in the best possible way.'
- Sharlene Teo, author of *Ponti*

'An immensely talented young writer ... [Emma Glass's] fearlessness renews one's faith in the power of literature.'
- George Saunders, author of *Lincoln in the Bardo*, winner of 2017 Man Booker Prize

'Electric and intoxicatingly honest.'
- Greta Bellamacina, poet, screenwriter and actress

'Utterly spellbinding. *Mrs Jekyll* is a crucial story about the paradoxes and paroxysms of modern womanhood, expressed with visceral intensity and dazzling originality. A true tour de force.'
- Ali Millar, author of *The Last Days* and *Ava Ana Ada*

For Deborah Orr

The late, great Deborah Orr was dying when she began to talk about her next book. She knew her diagnosis was fatal but she hoped she would have at least two more years in order to complete it. A novel. It was to be called *Mrs Jekyll* and as she lay in her hospital bed it was 'writing itself in my head'.

It was not to be, but CHEERIO is proud to have commissioned *Mrs Jekyll* by Emma Glass. We believe Deborah would be thrilled with the book and we have made a donation to St Martin-in-the-Fields Trust's 18 Keys project in her memory. This project is dedicated to providing a sanctuary and intensive support for female rough-sleepers.

To find out more please see their website, 18keys.org.

days are counted

Have you ever seen that advert on the telly, the one where an old couple are sitting outside on a bench? The old lady is knitting, needles clacking together, and she never takes her eyes off the stitch. Her husband is reading the newspaper and he stops to break off a square of chocolate, and he places it on her knee. He breaks off another square and pops it in his mouth. She doesn't stop knitting, but she raises her eyebrows and smiles.

When Charlie comes into the room with cups of tea, I have just seen this advert and I am unravelling. He smiles when he sees the tears in my eyes. He laughs at me when I cry at adverts. But he realises these tears are different. He can see my shoulders shaking; he can see the pain surging, the fingers of it crawling up my throat. My mouth is wide, wet, and it all spills out.

He is by my side, his arms are around me, he holds me hard

against his thick flesh. I wrack and rattle.

Hey, hey, hey, he muffles into my hair. What's all this?

It won't be us.

Of course it will.

It won't be us.

Rosy.

It is pointless struggling against him. I let him hold me, let my heart wear out against his steady thump. He taps me and soothes me like a cradled baby.

The tea is going cold.

Charlie is good at getting me through these moments. He's good at carrying on. We don't dwell.

We eat bowls of fruit and yoghurt. I hate peeling oranges. I can't bear pips and pith and the way the juice stains my fingertips. He does it all. He cuts the grapes. He cuts everything small so that it looks more than it is. If I eat a bowlful, even if it's only five grapes and three strawberries and a tablespoon of yoghurt, I have done it, I have eaten a bowlful of fruit and yoghurt, something I have done today, something I can write down on a list and put a tick in a box next to it. Little victory.

He has been getting a little belly. He won't let anything go to waste, like the mothers of picky children. His belly, like my head, is smooth and round and hairless.

night was cloudless

Impossible moon: I could pluck it out of the sky, wear it on a chain around my neck. Hanging low, kissing the falling leaves silver. The wind is rolling a crisp packet down the street. Everything crackles this time of year. The leaves under my feet. I can smell wood burning in the big, old houses, with fireplaces in every room, but no fires built; inefficient wood burners, not making much heat, but toasting mallows on the wind tonight. I breathe it in, walking home the long way round.

I'm all bundled up, hat and scarf, shoulders heavy with wool. Two ghouls go by shrieking happily, swinging little orange buckets full of sweets. Parents calling out after them. My heart stops, thickness of muscle in my throat when I come round the corner into webs with huge black spiders sitting in them, smothering the side of a house. I know they're not real but their enormousness threatens thousands of legs, of shadows twitching, touching. My flesh walks away to the other side of the street. I bump into a pirate, a witch and Iron Man; they all shout together TRICK OR TREAT and I say TRICK and they put a spell on me.

Eyes up to the sky, seeing stars. Lungs full of cold smoky air. I'm hungry for hot soup, hot sex, hot shower. Charlie is in the kitchen when I get home, stirring something on the stove with a wooden spoon. News on the radio is knitting his eyebrows together. I'm standing in the doorway taking off my boots and watching him. His glasses are steaming up. He puts the spoon down, comes over, puts his arms around me and kisses me. He tastes softly of stout.

Beef and ale stew? It smells delicious.

He makes mashed potatoes whilst I shower. We eat on the sofa watching a quiz show. He answers all the questions, biting his nails like he doesn't know if they're right, but they are. The only answer I can give is that *Sweeney Todd* was written by Stephen Sondheim. He asks me if I'm sure and I glare at him, daring him to make me sing.

We go to bed early.

Knead the flesh on his back. Need him inside me. He strokes my hair away from my face. Hour-long ravenous kiss.

pleasant dinners

Where are my shoes?

I'm on the carpet, on my hands and knees, head in the wardrobe, rummaging, dust flying up. I stick my head out for air and to sneeze. Make-up is probably all down my face now. Why do we always rush?

Don't wear any, he says, he grabs my ass, starts to caress; I kick him in the leg, not now, I say, we're already late.

Sally doesn't care, he says, she's probably hoping we'll cancel.

Oh, I don't think so, I say, pulling a shoe out of a bag and flinging it at him; he catches it with one hand and dusts it off. I sneeze, take a gulp of air and go back in to search for the other.

She definitely *does* want us to come, I say to the back of the wardrobe, she told me things are shit with Joe right now and she just wants to have a night with some adult company and

5

conversation, so they can feel like a couple again.

When I emerge with the other shoe, Charlie is sitting on the bed, holding my shoe, looking confused.

These don't match, he says.

We rush to the Tube. I am clomping in my heels. He pulls me along, bottle of red tucked under his arm, another thing from the back of the cupboard dusted off.

We stand on the doorstep in Wilton Square and I ring the bell. He takes my chin in his hand, turns my head, kisses me, says you look nice. I'm smiling brightly when Sally opens the door. Her face is flushed, her hot cheek melts my cold cheek as she leans in to kiss me. She seems so happy to see us and Charlie gives me a look that says something's up and I roll my eyes saying yes, that was what I was trying to tell you.

She takes the wine, coats, shuffles us into the living room which is lit with reading lamps and big candles.

Joe isn't long in from work, he's just getting changed. Drink?

Something smells delicious, I say. Can I help?

No, no it's all good, thank you, it's only lasagne.

She hands me a glass of wine, we sit down on the sofa; Charlie is standing, eyeing up the books on the shelves that cover every inch of wall.

Frank is asleep already, sending him to nursery on a Friday is brilliant, he wears himself out playing and running around, he was falling asleep in his dinner tonight. She shows me a photo on her phone, his little nose touching his spaghetti, eyes covered by a mop of milk-white hair that only toddlers have.

He's so cute, he looks so much bigger than when we last saw

him – when was that, three weeks ago?

Sally takes a gulp of wine. I can't believe it, time just goes, she says. But her eyes over the wine glass look at me and say it goes, but it also just stands still, it just stands still.

Charlie is reaching for a book so I jump up off the sofa and say I'm just popping to the loo; he drops his arm and goes and sits in my place next to his sister, I can hear him in his smooth, soothing voice asking how she's doing, what's new. I slip my shoes off at the bottom of the stairs and go quietly up. I tiptoe past Frank's room, go slowly past Sally and Joe's; the door is open a crack, I peer in; Joe is lying on the bed, scrolling on his phone, and this outrages me. I close the bathroom door loudly and turn on all the taps.

Joe and Charlie are talking avidly about the general election when I get downstairs. They are polishing their swords, speaking with sharp smiles, pushing points across pointlessly because we all know they vote the same way. I put my arms up defensively, say hello to Joe, kissing him very lightly on the cheek.

I'm going to give Sally a hand, I say, taking my wine with me.

Squeezing lemons for a salad dressing, she says he comes in from work every day, he'll kiss me, he'll kiss Frank, then he'll go upstairs for like twenty minutes and when I go up he's just lying there on his phone and when I ask him what's wrong he says nothing, says he just needs a minute, to decompress. But sometimes it's not twenty minutes, it's an hour. I call him down for dinner, he'll sit and eat with me, but it's all one-sided, he brings his phone with him. I tried not making him dinner the other night, see what he would do; he came down and started warming up a tin of soup! He's not mad, he's not sad, he plays with Frank, gets up with him at the weekends, but he won't really talk to me, or look at me, even.

Do you think something is going on at work? I ask, stealing an olive.

She shrugs. He usually tells me about work, he loves talking about books. I thought it might have been another woman, but he's not even sending messages on his phone; it's just scrolling, reading, watching videos, I don't know.

She drizzles the dressing. I think he's bored of me.

How could he be? Look at you, you're gorgeous, you work, you have a three-year-old, you cook, take care of the house, you're interesting and clever. I refill our glasses.

You're just saying that; you're my sister-in-law, you have to be nice to me, she says, smiling.

I'm being nice because it's true, because I think those things about you. I feel lucky Charlie has a sister like you — I wish I had a sister. Maybe Joe just needs to be reminded of how great you are.

I'm trying, she says, pointing with both hands to her waist, her dress. I feel like it's so much easier for him; he just has to go to work, he doesn't have to worry about dropping off at nursery, packing lunches, remembering birthdays, all the shit women do instinctively.

Mmmm.

But I can't really know what she means and I feel bad. I feel selfish. Charlie looks after me, I look after him. We're on the earth for each other. He cooks, I cook — OK, so I mostly clean, but he mostly plans; we both make money, it all goes in the same place.

Every day, he's the best bit of my day and if any of that changed I would just die.

Lasagne is delicious, chocolate mousse has split a bit.

Joe talks about work, nothing stressful there, he is editing an incredible new book, it will win a big prize, for sure. He talks about Frank, he is taking him to the Transport Museum tomorrow, so Sally can have a lie-in and go for brunch with her friends. He says it, but there isn't much behind his words, he's just sort of saying them; doesn't look at her, not once throughout the meal.

I help Sal with the dishes, Charlie and Joe go through to the living room with whisky, talking about a book he wants to borrow on environmental politics.

So, she says, what do you think?

I don't know. I don't know what to say.

He seems a bit distant, I say. A bit removed.

What should I do? she asks, sighing, leaning on the kitchen counter.

I think you should talk to him, ask him what is really going on, because there must be something.

Do you think Charlie will say anything to him? she asks, looking towards the living room.

I shrug. I'm not sure he has necessarily noticed anything is wrong. But I can ask him to, later, if you want me to.

She pours herself a whisky, offers me one, but I shake my head. She knocks it back.

We hug and kiss goodbye at the door. I look back as we go through the garden gate; Sally is waving and Joe has already turned and gone inside.

We hail a black cab, a treat, because we're both drunk and tired. We hold hands across the back seat, interlinking fingers.

If he didn't love me any more, would he tell me, or would he just take small, slow steps away from me until I realise and then it's too late?

by all lights and at all hours

Pawing, great big clumsy drunk hands, rubbing a finger under the collar of my dress, rubbing hands over my legs like my tights will dissolve if he rubs hard enough. I want to move faster than this, I don't feel sexy standing against our cold bedroom wall, eventually he'll see underneath my tights are my old cotton knickers and I will be reduced from someone he wants to have sex with to the only person he can have sex with and suddenly Sally is in my brain and she'll be there to rot and no, no, we are not the same as them. I push him away and his eyes sharpen, he is about to look hurt so I kiss the words into his ear, I'll be right back. I roll open my underwear drawer and grab anything that feels lacy and go into the bathroom. I brush my teeth, brush my hair, take off my tights and knickers and put on the black lacy pair, waistband high on my hips, stringy bit sitting between my buttocks. I stand on my tiptoes to see in the mirror. Don't ever really see my body in this way.

Feeling for my wetness fingers through the fabric he says you should wear these more often and I smile and say they ride up my ass and giggle and he flips me over quickly which makes me shriek and he says where let me see and he pulls the lace with his finger and puts his finger between my buttocks and slips in a little further until I say oh, and then he yanks my knickers all the way off. Warm silk of the tip of his penis pushes against me finds his way in we moan he goes louder when he hears me feel everything together the flesh and bone of him filling me up space between us disappearing until everything is ending with bliss beginning we can't hold on any longer the traces he leaves inside me when he comes are ribbons in every colour running and shimmering in the dark.

pace up

All rise.

We are up off our seats, we are giving it everything we've got, pushing against the resistance, beads of sweat dropping, you can hear them patter on the floor despite the music and heavy breathing and whirring wheels.

Add more if you can. Add MORE!

I obey. I reach down and turn it up another gear. My legs push on the beat, I glance at the clock, we're over halfway through, my water bottle is nearly empty, my towel is damp. Mirrored wall shows me the other spinners. I can't make out faces, we're doing it in the dark with disco lights, just shining foreheads, swinging ponytails, legs like insects, bowing, rounded knees, round and round.

Jerry is our reverend, he halts us with his hand, he says be seated, take rest. BUT KEEP THOSE LEGS MOVING.

Chemical Brothers. I like this one. I know where we're going. Sprint. Jerry's legs are silver bullets. Head bobbing with the beat. Takes me a little while to pick up speed racing against my own heart thump I can't help but bop along but I'm moving too fast I'm trying not to think forget the thought and the beat and keep up keep increasing the speed eyes on Jerry in those silver tights lights strobing as we go nowhere feeling the burn feeling every artery in my body pulse the blood rush air hushing through my lungs purely high as I rise I catch my eye in the mirror my teeth are bared my eyes are dark oh does my face look strange snarl smack crack and shriek my foot slips out of the strap.

Jerry is a silver streak of lightning bolting across the room. My other leg is still spinning. The class is leaning, taking a hairpin bend towards me.

Are you OK? Jerry asks, reaching down, beating the break, my leg stops, my hips shift. I'm fine, I say, no voice sounding, nodding, cherry-faced, burning up. He taps my shoulder, he hops back on his bike, brings everyone back on track. Some looks still linger in my direction. I strap back in, I'm going to finish this bitch.

I go over to Jerry at the end of the class and say sorry and thank you.

He says no worries, but you've got to strap in tight! See you next week.

See you then, I say.

I pack my sweat inside my jacket, zip all the way up for the short walk home.

I blend frozen fruit and a little juice, watch the berries blitz up and bleed. It pours a pleasing pink. I find the flaxseeds Charlie sometimes puts on his porridge, which he swears by but I don't know what they do. I put a teaspoon in and mix, regret it right away as I feel the seeds stick in my teeth.

Take my clothes off in the bathroom, all soaked through with sweat and sticking as they come off, skin trying to leave with them. I turn on the shower and let the steam build up. Press my cheek against the cool white tiles, press my bare back against the wall, let the cold turn me to aching stone. Sizzle when the hot water hits me. I exfoliate. I rub the gritty mixture over my neck, my collarbone, my breasts. Smells like grapefruit. Take care to scrub underneath my breasts, the place I sweat the most, feels raw and sore, dead skin rolling off in strands like residue from a rubber. My fingers rub around the curve of my breast. I feel it then. Press. I press again.

When Charlie comes home, I'm lying on the bed in my wet towel, my hair splayed across the pillow. He comes in and climbs on top of me and kisses me, I wince as the cold metal zip of his jacket tooths my soft bare belly.

Push him gently off, bring his hands together in mine and rub them together, feel the friction and the warmth collecting in his fingertips. I bring his hand to my breast and ask him if he can feel it. He looks confused. I say press firmly, can you feel some-thing?

I study his face, want to kiss the furrows of his forehead, watch them turn to trenches as he crushes my flesh.

Rosy, he says.

He wraps his arms around me, I rest my head on his chest and we lie there, bellies rumbling for lunch.

small sounds carried far

Poster paint and milk breath. We keep cosy on afternoons like this. Room so bright and yellow, the windows look like telly screens. We're watching the wind and rain but it's not real, it can't be, not when our little room is luminous, when their little faces are beaming. They sit cross-legged, hands on laps, mouths open, listening. I'm reading them a story bursting with magic, I slow down the pace of my words and watch their heads tilt, rosebud lips twitch with anticipation. My eyes glisten, I could cry at the purity of this moment, I would put each and all of them in my pocket: they are angels this way. I wet my lips and turn to the last page, I know my words ending will split their wonder at the seams, world ending, so I say them slowly, say them quietly and then gently close the book.

Silence doesn't last any longer, bums shuffle, fingers get

fidgety on the foam mats. I ask the class to tell me what they thought of the story, I toss the beanbag to them, and they take it in turns to pass it around, everyone says something, and I nod encouragingly. They think of things I would never have thought of, they choose words, the exact words of their wants. These are their daily gifts to me.

Shall we paint pictures of our favourite bits of the book? You can draw a character or a scene, it can be anything you like, but it has to say something about the story. Shall we do that?

Miss Harris has been setting up the painting tables so quietly and efficiently, I hadn't even noticed. The children stand and say thank you for the story Mrs Winter in unison; they turn and look at Miss Harris and she nods and says come on then and they scamp away and sit down at the tables and roll up their sleeves.

Jess? Could I ask you a favour? She comes to the front of the classroom, I talk quietly into her ear.

I have an appointment tomorrow morning with the GP. I don't really want to take a full day off, I think I'll be two hours, do you think you could manage the class until I get in? Mr Jones said it would be OK, but I don't want to put too much on you.

Yes, of course, Rosy. It's no problem, is the lesson plan done? she asks.

Yep, I nod, I thought we could do maths in the morning.

Sure, no problem. Is everything OK, are you OK? she asks.

Think so, I say. I chew my lip. She puts her hand on my shoulder.

I look at the bobbing cherubim heads. Ava looks up from her picture, pink protruding tongue, small as a cat's, steadying her concentration under her brown curls. She looks at us, she has a stroke of blue paint across her cheek. She says Mrs Winter, Miss Harris, are you doing paintings too? And we say yes and we each sit down at a table and pour our grown-up crippled imaginations in colours on sugar paper.

can't see what harm
it would do

Don't worry, I'll find you.

But it's a massive station and it's really busy!

You sound like Charlie, I say.

Urgh. I just hate getting public transport.

It's fine, I say. Just get a coffee, I'll be there in ten minutes, less than ten minutes now.

OK, I'm wearing my new camel hat and coat.

Sally! I know what you look like, don't stress, see you soon.

You've never known true responsibility until you've taken twenty-four five-year-olds on the Underground to the Science Museum, watched them go two by two in their tiny pink hi-vis vests, counted them, little hands holding little hands, still pudgy, haven't lost the baby fat yet.

You've never known true fear until you only count twenty-three.

Try not to panic, don't let it take hold, it'll close your throat. Relief chokes you when little fingers reach for yours, when you hear the sweet high excited voice that says, miss, look what I found! And the shiny penny clasped between thumb and forefinger held up for you to see, a treasure. So cross, you want to snatch it from them, so happy, you want to shower them with a thousand shiny pennies. Count them, count them twice. Your eyeballs go dry in their sockets because you'll never blink again in case you lose one. Keep your eyes peeled, become good at picking out faces in crowds. But Sally is right. Helps if they are wearing hi-vis vests. Or hats.

And what a hat! A golden felt fedora framing an anxious face, thick lashes flapping like wings as she turns her head side to side looking for me. Her caramel coat is long and belted, expensive. She holds a coffee cup in each hand, arms held out, awkward, to protect the coat from spills. She is immaculate and I am jealous. I feel shabby in my old navy duffel, I brush off lint that doesn't exist, run my fingers through my hair, feel around in my bag for some lip balm, but she sees me and tries to wave and the coffee starts to spill so I rush up and take the dripping cup from her, doesn't matter if it drips on me.

So. Many. Fucking. People, she says, as she kisses my cheeks. This is why I never take public transport. She smells powdered and flowery and I long for a speck of her glamour.

I reach into my pocket and pull out some balled-up tissues to wipe the coffee off my hands.

Sorry, she says, they never put the lids on these things properly. It's fine, I say, taking a sip and scalding my tongue. Thanks.

You look amazing. Only you could pull off a hat like that.

Oh, really? she says, touching the brim and blushing. Joe said it was a bit much.

Ignore him, it's fabulous. But I feel so underdressed, I thought we were just going for a look around the shops and then to the pub?

She links her arm with mine and we walk towards the platform.

We are, she says. But I kind of wanted to go somewhere else too. And I thought you'd be up for it so I've made a booking...

A booking for what?

Her face is half embarrassed, half mischievous.

A tarot reading.

A what?

Tarot – you know, to get our cards read, our fortunes and futures told.

Is she for real?

Our fortunes are disparate and will always be. But our futures, mine was going to be as long as hers, if not longer, and rich in love and living. Don't I deserve as much as she does?

She can't realise what she's asking me to do. She can't be that selfish.

I don't know what to say so I laugh and then I take a sip of my coffee.

I'm surprised at you, Sal, I didn't think you'd be the sort of person to believe in that stuff?

She blushes, embarrassed. She shrugs.

I don't know. I thought it might give me some insight into

what's going on with Joe. I mean, I don't have any fucking idea, but a mystic might... The woman doing readings tonight also has a shop in London, so she must be good! I thought it might just be a bit of fun. Thought it might take your mind off the surgery?

I was actually just thinking about her boots, wondering where she got them from, how much they cost, wondering how she found out about a tarot reading in Brighton, thinking about anything but the surgery. But there it is, mentioned, small, brought up somewhere loud and public where we couldn't possibly have a real conversation about it. Said because she has to say something, has to let me know she cares.

Sally, I'm fine, really, it's going to be fine.

She squeezes my arm tightly.

I know you will be fine, she says. I can't help but worry. It's a big thing to be going through.

And I have no choice but to go through it. It's not her body, not her shitty situation. Does she honestly want me to talk to her about this now? I try to hold my face and not show my glee at how blemished and sweaty she would look if I actually told her that I'm worried they might have to remove my whole breast if the disease has spread and my insides are black and rotting, that I'm worried I'll be infertile after chemotherapy, that we can't afford to have my eggs frozen and that I'm terrified I won't wake up from the anaesthetic.

She wears concern thickly, and for a split-second there is a flicker of expectation across her face.

I smile, take a sip of the now cool, bitter coffee and say thanks, it means a lot, you being here for me.

She presses her cheek to mine, her floral scent diluted with the saline of a stray tear. Any time, darling, she whispers.

Let's go have some fun, I say, and we link arms again and pick up our pace to the waiting train.

You know my mother would kill me if she knew I was going for a tarot reading.

Really? asks Sally.

Uh, have you ever met my mother? She'd go mad! Any kind of spiritualism beyond the Holy Ghost is not OK.

We find seats, take our coats off, settle in.

stared at each other
pretty fixedly

We shared a bottle of red wine at the pub. My lips are grape-stained and papery. I'm clutching a bag in my lap containing a red beret, which has been wrapped in tissue paper. Sally insisted it looked good on me (this was before the wine), insisted that I buy it so that we could wear our fabulous hats together. It started to rain, so it remains in the bag. Ridiculous, frivolous, I said when I tried it on again in the pub and Sally said you've got *cancer*, you can be as frivolous as you like. That prompted me to top up my glass and not hers.

We're sitting in a small room at the back of a bookshop. We had passed it earlier when we were looking round the shops, I noticed the dusty old books and dragon statuettes and thought to myself *Who buys this stuff?* and now I'm glad I didn't say it out loud to Sally because, when we arrived, her eyes lit up at the green neon sign that I hadn't noticed before saying TAROT READ HERE. Childlike excitement made her reach for my hand as we pushed open the door. A little bell tinkled.

Burgundy velvet curtains are parted for us to enter. The space is draped in different kinds of dark fabric, no windows, no walls, lit only by trays of candles on the floor. Sally sits at what looks like a stack of crates covered with fraying tulle, opposite a woman who has her eyes closed. A man with a ponytail brought a stool for me when Sally said I had to stay with her. He disappeared immediately, silently, a stagehand in a black T-shirt, blending with the dark. I sit behind Sally watching flames leap from wicks. I try not to breathe too deeply, afraid to move in case I knock one over and cause an inferno.

The woman's name is Jacqui and she is not what I expected. She's our age, she has braids down her back, she's wearing yoga leggings and her accent is South London.

Sally is tipsy and nervous and giggles now and again for no reason. She doesn't seem to understand when Jacqui tells her that the tarot cards won't predict her future.

Ten of Cups. Abundance, there is richness in your life, happy relationships, lots of them, you are well loved.

The Emperor. Who is this to you?

Sally takes the card, she turns, holds it out for me to see. She says, I mean he's definitely better-looking than Joe.

She laughs. Jacqui doesn't.

But yeah, that's Joe, my husband.

His force is impacting you; he is not allowing your power to emerge.

Well, yeah, I know that. What should I do about it?

Jacqui says the cards don't give us plain answers. But knowing that he is not empowering you, saying it out loud, gives you something concrete, something you can show him.

Sally says nothing.

Jacqui points to the third card. *Two of Swords*.

There is conflict, there are two sides pulling in opposite directions, a right thing and a wrong thing and you don't know which way to go.

I don't think I can leave Joe. I don't think we're there yet.

But this may not be connected to Joe. This could be guilt or shame. Swords are weapons, there could be pain somewhere that you know exists, but you shy away from.

There *could* be. Sally folds her arms. She is staring at Jacqui. She is unimpressed.

OK, well, thank you for that.

Jacqui turns the cards over and places them back in the deck. She says, you're welcome. You know, maybe next time we could try for a more targeted reading, you could send me some information in advance? It's like I said in my email, I am not a fortune teller. The cards give us insight. Even if there are things you already know, when taken together, the message of the cards can be enlightening.

Sally waves her hand around the space.

This is all just a bit... vague though, isn't it.

Jacqui shrugs.

I'm sorry you're disappointed, we can talk more about your issues, but I feel that you're not ready to embrace this kind of practice. You have paid for a second reading, is this for yourself, or for your friend? Would you like to go ahead with it?

Not sure what any more cups or swords will tell me, Sally says flatly. She looks back at me and whispers loudly shall we go back to the pub?

I look at Jacqui who is holding the tarot deck against her heart, watching a steady flame. She has a smattering of dark freckles across her nose and cheeks, high cheekbones; she is striking.

I'd like to have a turn, I say quietly. We're here now, you've already paid, we may as well. I stand and squeeze myself into the corner to let Sally pass. She is slightly irritated, but she takes my bag from me and tries not to huff too loudly as she sits on the stool. I sit opposite Jacqui, I am a little nervous; I interlock my fingers, place my hands in my lap, then on the table, she reaches out unexpectedly, she places her hand on mine to calm me. Her touch, her peace is wanted.

Tell me your name.

Rosy.

And what would you like the cards to reveal to you today, Rosy?

I'm not sure exactly, I say. I'm married, I'm a teacher, I don't have any children.

Yet, says Sally.

Jacqui shuts her eyes at this.

I have just been diagnosed with breast cancer.

I realise that I am telling myself this and not Jacqui.

Jacqui says, I'm sorry to hear that.

I smile and shrug and say I feel OK at the moment.

A scoff from Sally, now thoroughly cynical and bored. I ignore her.

I guess... I guess I'd like to know if I'm going to be OK? I know you can't predict the future or say anything for certain, but it's on my mind.

Jacqui nods. Let's see.

She shuffles the deck with a quick flick of her thumbs, then places them on the table between us. She spreads them across the surface, touching them delicately with long, elegant fingers. She teases a card from the centre and turns it over.

Six of Cups. The longing for a familiar and happy past. This makes sense when you're faced with a challenge, like sickness. You may feel uncertain about the future, so you are looking back through time, hoping you'll find answers. Could you have done something differently? You ask yourself this question often. You search for the meaningful moments that if you hold in your mind you can will into the present. This may not be possible, but keeping these memories close can be useful when you are going through a hard time.

Not true. I've never asked myself that. But I do ask myself if I deserve this. I'm not suffering yet, but I know I will and should I just embrace it, because that's what it costs?

I realise she's looking at me, waiting for me to react, but I'm not ready to speak, so I nod in acknowledgement, and she draws the second card.

The High Priestess.

Jacqui is smiling, she leans closer to me, our foreheads nearly touch as I lower my head to look at the card. Pearlescent beauty, straight-backed, unbending, the moon at her feet.

I had a feeling this card would come tonight. She is the Divine. A symbol of intuition and the subconscious. She tells us to look inwards and trust our own power.

I shake my head. No, this card isn't for me, this is surely Sally's card. I turn towards Sally, now just a shape of a woman in the darkness.

Well, yes, this could apply to Sally, she is divine for sure – but she didn't show up for her. She showed up for you.

She points to the serene face.

This card is for you. This *is* you. You may not feel this way about yourself but look inwards. Trust your feelings, embrace what is there, the flesh and the meat, but trust that there is more. Not just the physical, but the spiritual. The moon. You can have it all. Your inner reflections can open you up to experiences you may not have had before, may never have wanted before.

I feel her breath on my face as she speaks, her words hang heavy in the air, her eyes are melting wax in the candlelight. My cheeks are hot, I am fixed to the spot.

The last card.

Look, this one has something it wants to share with you. She points to one which has emerged by itself.

She turns it over slowly.

Her smile vanishes.

I sense Sally shifting behind me, her movements cause the flames to flicker, shadows crash like waves.

The warmth in my face melts away.

Horrible horns. Face the colour of dried blood. He hovers

over shackled humans, his flaming torch touches the earth. Can't help but shudder.

Jacqui whispers, don't worry. *The Devil* doesn't mean quite the same thing here as in other religions. He is upright. He signifies temptation, urges, the darkness within everyone. We use his presence as an opportunity to be reminded of how powerful temptation can be. Embracing our urges can be freeing, but we must be cautious not to lose ourselves in the darkness. No one can live without consequence.

Her hands hover above the drawn cards. I want her to reach out and take my hand again, but she doesn't, she is looking behind me. At first, I think she is looking at Sally, but when I turn around, Sally is gone. The space behind me feels hollow and oddly cold. I look back at Jacqui, but her gaze remains over my shoulder. Her face is changing, furrows slash across her forehead one by one, her eyes are watering.

Jacqui?

She blinks, her eyes come back to mine.

Are you OK?

She nods slowly.

Your friend left, she says.

I didn't notice, I say.

She leans towards me, bringing her face close to mine again. She whispers, but you are not alone.

What do you mean?

There is someone else here with you.

I don't understand.

She grabs my hands. She closes her caramel eyes to let

golden tears drip.

You will. The cards have been very powerful for you tonight. This doesn't happen often. I think I can help you, Rosy.

Help me? Help me with what?

Harness your power.

What power? Is she mad?

I pull my hands away from her.

I'm sorry, I say. I don't know what you mean. This was meant to just be for fun. And now it's just...

Please, don't close yourself off, not like Sally. This could enrich you. This could save you.

Save?

I shake my head. I put on my coat.

Thank you, but I need to go now.

She stands with me. She holds out a card. *The Empress*. I don't know what it means, don't care what it means.

Here, she says, please just take this. I have a shop in London. Please come and see me. I can help you, I'm sure that I can.

Her eyes are honest. I hesitate. Then I take the card and jam it in my coat pocket. I say goodbye and leave.

Sally is waiting for me outside the shop. She is stamping her feet in the cold and smoking a cigarette.

Well, that was fucking weird, she says. Sorry. I would have stayed but that woman was... She kept looking over at me, but it was like I wasn't there, she was staring through me. And then *The Devil* just finished me off. And that guy with the ponytail? What was he even doing there? What a creep. Right, back to the pub?

I take the cigarette from her and take a long drag.

laboured to relieve suffering

Clear margins. I tell him he deserves a gold star. Charlie tells him we can't thank him enough, shakes his hand, sighs and sits back in the chair beside my bed where he has been sitting for three days in the same jeans and jumper, everything about him creased. And now this news and he's running his hands through his hair, letting the smile take over his face, unwrinkling.

I'm up to my eyeballs in anaesthetic and analgesia. Everything is soft and white: the sheets, the light, there is a halo hovering over the surgeon's head, there are wings sprouting from his scrubs, he is smiling, saying what will happen next but it all just sounds like soft music to me. I let my eyes close, and I sleep away.

I'm sore. Dressings covering my wound for a few days. My mother is coming to stay. She used to be a nurse; she wants to help. Charlie can only take so much time off work and I don't feel ready for him to see just yet. I don't know what I'll look like. Still all swollen, still all yellow and purple.

I sit on the edge of the bath, my mother has to get down on her knees, I feel bad, she creaks and groans but she won't let me stand in case I faint. She said the dressing coming off will make me feel funny and she's right, I've never been good with blood or sick or anything. The gauze has been laid out. She calls it her sterile field but it's just a paper towel out of a plastic pack.

She peels back the dressing gently, bumps go up like chicken skin, hairs get caught, I bite the flesh on the inside of my lips and close my eyes.

You can do it faster, Mam, I just want it to be over with.

I hold onto the side of the bath, gripping tightly, breathing through my nose hard, pushing air out, sucking it in. The dressing coming off is heavy, curved, crusted. It smells like in-between sweaty toes.

She inspects the layers of silicone mesh and gauze and tape, holds them up to the light, pokes them with her finger.

It's dry, she says. That's good. We don't want it to be all wet.

She drops the dressing into the bin under the sink. She brings her face close to the wound. I turn my head away. I don't want to see it.

It looks healthy, she says, it's pink, the edges are together. A bit crusty though. Will you let me clean it?

Then my legs start to go.

Can you do it quickly? I want to lie down.

She's there with the wet gauze, a little white square, she's squirted something on it.

It's just saline, it won't sting.

She dabs it, she's being as gentle as she can but the fibres get caught in the crust and drag, like a snagged nail when you catch it in wool, makes you suck the air up through your teeth.

Sorry, sorry, she says.

I let go of the side of the bath and put my fingers into her soft white hair. I play with the little tufts and cry quietly whilst she cleans away the dried blood from the wound. She's crying too.

She runs me a bath – no salts yet though, just warm water. She helps to wash my hair because it is too painful to lift my arm.

Reminds me of when you were little, she says, cupping my forehead with her hand to stop shampoo running into my eyes, as she pours water from a little plastic jug over my head.

It usually annoys me when she reminisces, happier to remember me as a half-formed human, small, soft, blind like a newborn pink-skinned creature, wrapped in a towel, sat on her knee as she rubs moisturiser into my arms and legs and combs my hair, keeping me brand new. But I let her this time, let her wrap me up, help me into bed, hold my hand. I let her tell me it will be all right.

She imagines me bringing her fruit baskets and flowers and soup, opening the window an inch for air, sitting by her bed, telling her stories, gossiping, anything to get her mind off it, maybe bringing a baby, a grandchild, to hold in her weak arms, to love with her strong old heart, she can picture it all, because that is how it is meant to be. Meant to wave goodbye, leave quietly, make room in the world for the young.

She gets up onto the bed beside me and tucks herself into

the recesses of my spine and knees. She is warm and round and boosts my bony back like pillows. We are giggling when Charlie comes in. He leans against the doorframe, listening to her.

When you were little, really little, not long walking, your father was painting the bedroom and you wanted to see what he was doing, so I took you in there and your face lit up when you saw the ladder. So, your father picked you up and sat you on the bottom step where your little feet dangled in their little shoes; you were so cute, but you didn't want to sit, you were holding your arms up and kicking your legs out, reaching backwards for the balance bar.

So, your father picked you up and you grabbed on with your little chubby hands and he let you go and you held on and swung your little legs back and forth and you were chuckling away to yourself, hanging from this bar, but after about half a minute your arms got tired and you started to cry.

So, he picked you up and put you down on the step, we were watching you, you were looking back up at the bar, you toddled down off the step and realised you could reach the bar yourself, so you held on, tightly, with those little hands and swung yourself from the bar, laughing away, little legs kicking. But soon enough your arms started to ache again and you started to cry, got yourself up but couldn't get down; I fetched you down, but back you went, me and your father always used to laugh about that, every time the ladder came out.

Charlie goes to make tea. Mam strokes the top of my arm gently.

And look at me now, I say with a little laugh in my voice.

Can't even lift my arms up to wash my own hair. But I'll be all right, Mam, they cut it out and then I'll have chemo and I'm young and healthy. I'm not worried.

She nods and the tears stream down her face. That's what I'm praying for, she says. Praying every day.

strain of gaiety

I stick my arm out to be unbandaged. My nurse today is Patrice. She has a thick rope of black silken hair down her back, looks like it weighs more than she does. Her movements are quick, pin-sharp, efficient. She wipes the hub of my line and draws the blood before I've finished telling her how I feel today (like shit), how I've been sleeping (badly), what I've been eating (nothing). She attaches a syringe and injects the antiemetic. I watch her thumb on the plunger. I don't see it move but in three minutes the syringe is empty.

You just relax, she says, tapping my shoulder. I'll just go and speak to the doctor about your bloods, I think he was happy with the results from yesterday, and then we can start your chemo, OK?

Thanks, Patrice.

Thanks, Patrice, echoes Charlie. He stands and says, right, I'll go and get the coffees then, shall I?

I rest my head against the back of the chair and close my eyes.

Sure, I say, nothing for me, thanks.

Oh, go on, it's going to be a long day, plus, no offence to the tea lady but the stuff she brings round is rank.

I shrug and say I don't really mind it.

He huffs and says, fine, suit yourself. He stands in the middle of the bay and says loudly, ladies! I'm doing the coffee run! What can I get you?

Oooh! You're too kind, Charlie, I'll have a cappuccino please, says Madge.

Well, if you're going anyway, says Megan, I'll have a skinny latte, please.

I can't let you pay again, Charlie, let me give you some money, says Audrey, folding a ten-pound note and stretching her arm out towards him. She shuffles forward in the chair trying to reach him.

Now now, Audrey, don't you worry about that, he says, helping her back into the chair. It's my treat, I'd like to do it, plus Rosy is a cheap date, he says, winking. Their laughter is cackly, crackly and witchy. I can't help but smile.

Patrice? Can I get you anything? he says, tapping her lightly on the shoulder.

No thank you, she says, but it's very kind of you to offer.

She is busy untangling lines, spiking the hanging bags of chemo, running the bright red fluid through the lines, redder than blood, thinner than water. I try not to think about it.

Charlie gives me a kiss and says, I'll be right back.

You've got a good one there, says Madge, he's a real saint. You're lucky to have someone who looks after you so well.

I nod. I am lucky, I say.

How long have you been married? asks Megan. She's not as old as the others, I would guess she's in her early fifties, she doesn't wear a wedding ring, but she has a faint tan line where one used to be. She's never brought anyone with her before. Never been collected by anyone either. She wears jeans and flip-flops even though it's cold out.

Five years, I say, playing with my wedding ring, which has become loose. The skin on my finger is dry and flaking and irritated. Maybe Megan had the same trouble and just took hers off. Maybe I'll ask her one day.

And kids? she asks.

Audrey says loudly, no, dear, they don't have kids. The regret in her mouth smacks against her false teeth. Not yet.

Megan is shocked and then annoyed by Audrey's interjection.

I shrug and say it just hasn't happened for us yet, I don't really know why. And obviously now isn't a good time to be thinking about starting a family.

Megan nods sympathetically.

Madge says, but you have to think about the future, Rosy, stay positive. You'll be fine, and think of Charlie, he'll be a wonderful father. Time will get away from you. Young people think they have all the time in the world, but what are you – thirty-five, thirty-six? If I were you I'd be trying for a baby as soon as the doctor told me I was good to go...

Especially if I had a husband as good-looking as Charlie! says Audrey.

This time the two of them cackle, this time they are not witchy, just witches, bitching.

Megan tells me to take no notice of them.

I never do, I lie, smiling.

But I do.

Dr Carson says your bloods are fine, says Patrice. She connects my line up to the bag and starts the infusion.

Charlie spends the day being charming and chatting. I watch him being sweet, fetching pillows and glasses of water and telling jokes. He's particularly attentive to Audrey. He finds something familiar in her. Her cloudy eyes brighten when he speaks. He will never tell me but he misses his mother terribly.

weeping like a woman
or a lost soul

The room is arranged for a talk, with rows of chairs facing a white-painted brick wall.

We use it as a projector screen, she says, handing me a mug of tea.

People come and give lectures, sometimes we hold book launches and the authors give readings and do panels and stuff. There's always something going on, got to make it work somehow. She sits next to me in the back row.

This is for tomorrow, she says, gesturing towards a table stacked with the same purple book.

A medium, his name is Sven, he's mostly full of shit but people really like him.

Oh, I say, a little surprised by her candidness.

I mean, I wouldn't call him a charlatan *exactly*, but he goes for the low-hanging fruit, you know, tells people what they want to hear.

Huh. Maybe I should recommend him to Sally, I say, smirking.

Jacqui laughs, a little surprised by my cattiness.

How can you tell if someone is genuine? I ask.

She turns to me, puts her hand on my shoulder and says, I'll never use your fear against you and I'll never ask you to come to me unless you want to. Like I said when we first met, I think I can help you, but I don't expect you to trust me blindly. It will take time.

I don't know what kind of help I need, but I know that I like the warmth of her hand on my shoulder, the softness of her voice, that I want to be around someone who will see something other than sickness, weakness. I take *The Empress* card out of my pocket and place it on my knee. I smooth out the crumpled edges.

I don't know why, but I've been carrying this with me since that night in Brighton. What is she?

Mother, creator, says Jacqui.

My heart sinks. Always comes back to that.

You don't have children? she asks.

Her hand hasn't left my shoulder.

No. No children. We don't even have a cat.

The Empress isn't just about pregnancy. She nurtures, she inspires beauty and abundance and shows us that if we are receptive to change, we can flourish. She wasn't drawn during your reading, but she was the card sitting between Sally's and yours, and when I turned her over, I felt that she had come for you.

I shift in my seat so that her hand will drop from my shoulder.

I doubt her, I doubt this woman, her serenity, her reaching. She doesn't know me. If she did, she'd know I'm about to decay, I may die, and a bunch of illustrations on cards and allusions isn't going to do anything to help me. I stare far away into my cup.

I don't know what it's like for you, she says. Can't even pretend to know. But I can be here, I can listen.

I have so little to say.

ecstasy of listening

We were the most beautiful creatures on Earth that morning. He was, but I was too. We were peaceful. We were looking at each other, touching each other, hands moving over bare skin, fingers dipping with contours, coming to know the bones of the bodies, coming to know the insides. Deep kisses covering every inch of flesh, the warmth and softness of mouths.

We had spent the night in sleeping bags on the living room floor. We woke with the sun rising, the birds singing. I could have lain there forever with my head on his chest, listening to him transform the empty room into our home. We would sweep away the dust, we just had to imagine, had to look past the magnolia walls, the pipes rusted at the joins and painted thickly and thickly with white emulsion — we'd box them in, we'd knock out the wall to open up the space.

I thought the spell would break when he climbed out of the sleeping bag, but he zipped me up inside, kissed my forehead and my eyelids and my lips and said stay there. He stretched out, reaching up, just touching the ceiling, he yawned and smiled. He took a tape measure out of his backpack, put a pencil behind his ear and started measuring the room. I watched the way he moved, studied the curves of his muscles as he crouched or knelt or stood or stretched. He stuck the tip of his tongue out when he concentrated.

My mother said, but you're not even married yet and his sister said, but it is so small.

He came back to me, his body cold, hairs curling, he lay between my legs and we warmed again. He said to me I know it's small, I know it's not much and I said no, no it is so much, it is everything, it is ours.

here is another lesson
to say nothing

Stayed last night to finish the display and Charlie was furious because I didn't tell him I was going to be late. I was busy, time got away from me. I enjoyed being alone, I sang along to the radio, I sipped my tea, I climbed onto the bench to reach the board, stapled reams of paper and corrugated borders, chose the colours myself, placed the pictures myself, where I thought they looked best, the way I thought the children would like their work to be displayed.

What do you think, Jess? Do you like it?

It looks great, she says. But I wish you'd told me you were going to stay late. I would have stayed to help you.

I know, but I wanted to do it by myself. You've been doing so much to help lately, I wanted it to be something that I managed on my own.

You don't need to manage on your own, Rosy, we're a team!

I know, I say. I give her hand a little squeeze.

The photographer comes over and says, right, ready when you are, Mrs Winter.

Perfect, I say. Jess, do you want to get them in their rows? I'm just going to pop to the toilet.

Their excited chattering voices follow me across the corridor, I close the door on them. I lean over the tiny sinks to check myself in the mirror. I have a lump in my throat. Mr Jones said it couldn't wait any longer, couldn't pay the photographer to come back a second time, didn't want the kids to miss out. Said I didn't have to be in the picture if I didn't want to, completely understandable, could just take the picture with Jess instead.

But Jess isn't their teacher.

Add a dab of blusher and some pink to my lips. Smooth out the creases in my headscarf. I'll be able to look back at the picture one day and say to Charlie, do you remember when I lost all my hair? And he'll say, it was so long ago now, I can hardly remember. The thought puts a little smile on my face, and I leave it there for the picture.

Back in the classroom the children are waiting in neat rows, only Abel is picking his nose and Sabrina is fidgeting, but they stop when they see me, all their little faces beaming. I am so delighted, I start clapping.

Good job, everyone! Now, where shall I stand?

By me, miss! says Miles from the centre of the back row.

We've got it all planned, says Jess. We'll do the first picture with our biggest and best smiles and the second picture as silly sausages.

I love it, I say. Great idea!

I squeeze between Miles and Maya. Jess kneels on the end of the front row.

Right, are we all ready? says the photographer.

Miles is cupping his face with his hands.

Miles? Hands down please, we're doing our best smiles now.

But he doesn't bring his hands down. I bend to look at him but he turns away from me and then I see Maya doing the same thing, hands to her face, turning away from me.

Maya?

Mohammed is standing in front of me, steps away, pinching his nose.

What's going on?

Ollie pinches his nose and says, POOOOH! What's that SMELL?

Jess stands up and says, class? What's going on?

Miles says, sorry, miss, but there's a horrible smell.

Coming from where?

The children, all of the children, point at me.

last ingredient required

She finds me sobbing my heart out in the toilets. Headscarf off, balled up, covered in mucus. I don't care.

Rosy, let me get you some water.

I don't want any water. I want to be left alone.

They're only little, they don't understand, she says, slumping down to sit next to me, knees to our chests, backs against the wall.

But they're right. I do smell. I just don't notice it any more. Jess sounds like she's breathing through her mouth.

It's burdock root. I make burdock root tea. It's meant to help with inflammation and I read about this woman who was basically cancer-free after drinking it for three months. So I've been drinking it. A lot of it.

I start to laugh. Laugh hard. Knees slide down and I roll onto my side, tears spreading out, a puddle trapped between my cheek and the tiles.

Rosy?

She shakes me. Pulls me up.

What's so funny?

I smell like a mouldy sweet potato. I've been drinking this shit for two weeks. Because of something I read on the internet. I've lost my mind.

She doesn't laugh. She wraps her arms around me. I'm so hot and sweaty, I feel like I'm going to faint. But she doesn't let me go.

startling blasphemies

When I slammed the door, he was standing there with his arms open, palms up. Was he giving, was he taking away? What can he offer me now?

The fights are ugly, and the neighbours know. Sitting in their flats, one eye on the shaking pane of glass above their doors, one eye looking for the remote control so they can finally turn their tellies down.

Wind screams and spits in my face as I walk down the street to the bus stop. Nothing is stopping me. The bus crawls for no reason at all. I could walk there faster. I used to be able to walk there faster, now the bus rolls and jolts, rolls and jolts and now it rattles the bones in my bloodless body.

Let it, then.

Have patience, then.

I close my eyes, breathe deeply in through my nose, try to block out the buzz and hum thrumming thrum.

When I open my eyes the bus has stopped, the engine is off, it is tucked behind another bus, behind another bus, behind another. The lights are bright on and the automatic announcement says BELONGINGS WITH YOU THIS BUS TERMINATES HERE PLEASE MAKE SURE YOU TAKE ALL YOUR BELONGINGS WITH YOU THIS BUS. I catch the driver's eye in his rear-view mirror and he's hoping I will just get up and go. He's deciding whether I'm drunk or on drugs or homeless, and just seeing the look in his eye, I can tell he's been watching me for a while and he really, really doesn't want to get out of his acrylic box. Keep the animals out.

I've slept all the way to Trafalgar Square. I say sorry and wave and he nods hesitantly and opens the door for me. I used to want to shout I'VE GOT CANCER! But the urge has eroded. I do have cancer, but he may have heart disease, arthritis, diabetes or epilepsy. What we both have is a life worth living, so we'll get on with it just fine, quietly.

Legs strengthened by the little sleep propel me to the place. The street is wet and shiny, but I don't remember it raining. The wind hasn't followed me but a chill curls around my meatless bones. Thankful for my cardigan.

I knock softly on the window. I can see Jacqui standing by the till, perfect posture, silver hoop earrings shining as she throws her head back laughing, I don't know who she's with, can't see their face. The lights inside are glowing. I knock again, a little louder, and then wave when she turns. Her eyebrows rise and she smiles widely. I see her mouth saying, here's Rosy. She grabs a set of keys from the desk and comes to the door to let me in.

Hi! You made it! Come on in!

Incense burns. Sandalwood and sage tingles my nostrils. I breathe in deeply. What a joy it is to smell something other than myself. Jacqui takes both my hands and pulls me into the shop.

How are you, she says, you look well, you look well, I'm so glad you could come, I was worried you wouldn't. It's important that you came, I'm glad you felt like you could, I'm glad you felt well enough. Is Sally with you? Good, that's good actually. We've got *balance* here tonight, the energy is well balanced. Come, can I take your coat?

I'll keep it on for now, if you don't mind, I'm a little bit cold.

Of course, of course, let's have some tea. But look, I want you to meet Katrina. Katrina, this is Rosy.

Katrina is standing by the till. She is young and beautiful. Her cropped copper hair is shimmering in the low lights. She has green eyes lidded with the thickest black eyelashes and the first thing I ask her is what mascara she uses.

She laughs like a little ringing bell.

Sorry, I say. I'm just so jealous of anyone with long eyelashes. I miss mine.

She nods.

They'll grow back, she says. She smiles like she knows a secret.

I hope so, I say. But I don't sound hopeful. I look around for Jacqui; she's downstairs boiling the kettle.

Katrina is looking at me. I feel self-conscious. I fold my arms, I want to make myself smaller. I look like a boulder in my big grey coat, concealing layers of vests and sleeves and scarves.

I wonder if she can smell me.

How do you know Jacqui? I ask, taking half a step away from her.

Oh, Jacqui is just amazing, isn't she? We met a few years ago. I was here, looking for a book on healing, we just sort of hit it off... she helped me.

She hasn't even blinked. Her eyes melt away the make-up on my face. She sees me sallow, hollow.

Jacqui didn't tell me anyone else was coming tonight, I say, looking down at my hands.

Oh yes, says Katrina. It can't just be the two of you. It's safer with three. And Jacqui thought it would be good for you to meet me, in case you needed reassurance.

She reaches out and touches my arm. I try to stop the wince from writhing across my face but it's too late. She withdraws her hand like she's touched a stove.

I'm sorry! she says, her pink, balmy mouth falling, cheeks flushing with worry.

It's fine, I say. I'm a little sore there.

She closes her eyes for a moment, like she's remembering. She nods. Her eyelashes lie in delicate ebony fringes across her cheeks.

Jacqui! she calls, without opening her eyes. Are you ready for us?

Come down! we hear her say from below. I look down at the floor and see faint light lifting through thin cracks in the floorboards, like straight gold strands of hair.

I follow Katrina down the steps, I watch her body curve

from side to side in that long, black, fitted dress, something I would never wear, even before, but now I wish I could feel that long, single piece of soft fabric falling against my skin.

It's not like it was before. No stacks of books, no rows of chairs, no lights on. Just a handful of candles on the coffee bar, one in the centre of a small circular table in the middle of the room. The corners of the room are indistinguishable, thick with shadows. My eyes adjust to the dark and then I see black velvet curtains hanging. Too heavy to flutter but they look like they are moving.

Candlelight, a draughty basement, a mouse. Is there someone else here? I take slow steps towards the curtains, reach out to draw them back, but Jacqui says not yet, Rosy, not yet, come and have some tea. I turn away and feel eyes on my back, but Jacqui says there's no one else here, it will just be the three of us tonight. She smiles at me and Katrina, hands me a cup with no handle. Jasmine and mint, she says, to stimulate our spirits. I breathe in the fragrant steam, try to absorb the heat to keep the chill from walking up my spine.

Shall we sit?

We sit snugly around the table, our knees brush, I look at Jacqui and she nods. She says, we must be this close, to connect.

Before we start, we should speak aloud our intentions. Jacqui looks at me, then Katrina.

Rosy, tell us why you came here tonight.

Now I feel hot. But I don't want to take my coat off. I want to dissolve on the spot. Hot tears spring. Jacqui takes my hand. It's OK, she says, soothingly. It's OK. Katrina takes my other hand. The smell of jasmine is overpowering. I want to be sick. We are too close to each other, too close to the candle. I am sweating. I pull my hands away and take off my hat. Thin tufts of hair are stuck to my head. I stuff my hat into my coat pocket. I take my coat off. Katrina sees the ache in my movements as I shrug my left arm out of the sleeve. I don't try to hide the pain now; I can't hide the stain on the scarf wrapped around my arm. I take a deep breath through my nose. The sickly smell of my wound mingles with mint. We can all smell it. Katrina and Jacqui close their eyes and breathe with me.

I'm here, I say, voice catching.
I'm here because I am dying.
I start sobbing.
I'm here because I want to know
Know if the end is
The end
Or if there is some thing some spirit
Some way of speaking
Will he hear me when I'm gone?
I don't want
To die
I have prayed
I am in pain
I did what they said
My body won't hold me any more
Heart pumps nothing
No blood
Flapping useless flesh

I feel it folding closed in my chest.

I try to suck air through my clogged nostrils. I wipe my eyes on the heels of my hands. I close my eyes and go on.

But something courses through me still

Energy

Will

Stubbornness

I hold on

Clinging

Tell me there is something else

Tell me—

They hear me swallow. They place their hands gently on mine.

Katrina says that she is here because she was sick once, like I am. I had chemotherapy, she explains, and it nearly killed me. I came to Jacqui, we channelled my pain. I spoke to those in spirit and they said it wasn't my time. I'm in remission and I want the same for Rosy.

She hears me gasp. She opens her eyes. I grip her hand tightly. Is she for real? She smiles at me, nodding, tears in her eyes too.

Jacqui says, I'm here because I believe in Rosy's power. I believe she will hear voices in spirit and they will guide her to comfort. To life.

Candlelight carries the same smile across our faces. We share warmth through our interlaced fingers. We breathe in. We breathe out. Our breath causes the flame to flicker rhythmically. We bow our heads.

Rosy. When you are ready you must go behind the curtain.

You must ask the spirit to come to you.

I look up at Jacqui. Her pupils are long black holes. Her face has lost softness, her cheeks are grey, her mouth is a concrete line.

Katrina keeps her head down and whispers, you must. You mussst.

I join their hands and push my chair back, stand up on my own wooden legs.

I stand in front of the velvet curtains. I wait. I listen. There is nothing. I reach out and touch the rich fabric. It is soft, heavy. I draw it back to reveal a little wooden chair. I step into the space and run my hand around the sides, all black, all velvet, a little box, with just enough room to stand or sit.

I sit.

Jacqui says, close the curtains.

I close them.

Jacqui says, don't be scared, Rosy.

But I am.

Candlelight doesn't reach me. Cut off. Senses deadened by thick dark. Sound of their breathing so faint, like their lungs are tired, like they'll stop soon. Swallow down the panic like sick. Focus on bringing air in and out of my body. Focus on my body. My body. Failing body. I unwrap the stained scarf, the sodden bandage and expose my wound. Even in this blackness I can see its outline. Hump. Hive. Heaves as I breathe. Protrudes proudly. It is the only part of my body that feels alive. Palpitating, proliferating close enough for the curtains to brush the hairs on my arms and my neck make them stand on end. I suddenly sense some thing, some one, some other.

Is this the spirit?

Someone is humming. It might be me. Someone is saying bring me to life. It might be me. Someone is humming, it's not me, someone is saying bring me to life, it's not me. I am rocking backwards and forwards, the chair creaks beneath me. An ashen body on the floor. It crawls. Bring me to life. Reaches out with brittle fingers, grasps my ankle, my mouth is open, screaming, the sound is a lost downpour in the sea. Bring me to life. Hand sliding up my leg, snatches my stomach and slithers towards my throbbing throat. Bring me to life. Fingers in my eyes I cry out I scream I shake the chair breaks I am brought to the floor I am writhing on my knees.

this creature stealing like a thief

Birth is wet
    Brand-new fingers
    Peeling back mucosa
    Pressing down on muscle
    Emerging from the wetness of mouth

    Spit me out

    Tangled in sinew
    Tearing
    Soaked in saliva
    Must have been a gobful
    Mouth to mouth
    Lips leave feeling full

Looking up from the floor
Black hole is the first thing
I see

Skin prickling
Pruritic
Touch me so that I know I am alive
Crawling towards the husk of you
Pull off your clothes
Your wasted flesh falls out of the wool
Easily
My arms stretch into your sleeves
My feet step into your shoes
Kneel next to you
Put my hands on your body
Run fingers over your ribs
Pass me a blanket
Cover you
Cloak you
Keep quiet
Sleep well.

In the outside
I breathe
With my mouth wide open
Let air in
Let lungs lubricate
Open up the little pockets

Stuff them wide
Capacity unknown but bet I can run
These are not the right shoes
Too small
Look at these perfect feet
No hard skin
Nothing dry
I stand on one leg
Lift my foot out of the shoe
Lift my sole
Run it up this smooth shin
Newborn silken skin
I walk
These exquisite legs take me to the place
Faces in the window
A face I know
Looking out hard
Misting up the glass
A face I could take
Or I could leave it
Takes a sip of gold from a jar
And I have to taste it.

Touch the door
Do I push
Do I pull
Painted newly
Emulsion tacky

Sticky sticky
To my fingertips
Weight of the wood is taken
By a man
Leaving
With a woman
He holds the door for me
Eyes go over my face
My exposed collarbone
He smiles
Woman sees and scowls
First smile spreads showing my white teeth
Pearls
Pisses her off.

Find the face
He is still looking out of the window
I push away empty glasses with my elbow
Stand next to him
Rest my hands on the ledge
Splay my long fingers

I ask him who he is looking for

He doesn't hear me

My voice is fizz
My voice is crackles

Shift the sputum

I ask him who he is looking for

It comes out like curling smoke

He turns his head

He looks
He is looking
In my eyes
In my smile
Confusion crimps the corners of his mouth
He wants to say, don't I know you

But he doesn't
He looks
Searching
For something he can't find
Can't find it
He looks out of the window
Across the street
Lights are off in the shop

He sighs
Looks at his watch
Sips the pint

Looks at me
Smiling at him

We haven't met before, have we?

I shake my head

He looks at my bare legs
My bare shoulders

Aren't you cold?

I shake my head

I came from somewhere warm
Who are you waiting for?

My wife

Puts his glass down

I watch the tiny bubbles
The foamy top
The colour is beautiful
The colour of my hair

Your wife

Lift my fingers
Circle the rim of the glass
Dip my finger in it
Cold
Drip it in my mouth
Suck the tip
Of my finger
Fizz on my tongue

His eyes turn hot on me
Hot
Turn me on

Would you like a drink?

I nod

He smiles
I'll be right back

One, two, three, four, empty glasses
He spills some from the full glasses of beer he brings from
the bar

Tell me about your wife

His face goes red

She went in there
He points to the shopfront
Windows black dark

What's in there?

I don't know
My wife isn't well

I drink the beer
Too fast
Drown my mouth
Teeth roaring with the delicious chill
Bubbles up my nose
Makes my eyes sparkle

I stretch to feel the liquid drip into my empty belly

He watches me glitter

I put my hand on his arm
I'm sorry to hear about your wife
She'll be OK

He looks at me
His face changes with anger
Yeah?
How do you know?

You know my wife?

I shake my head
I shrug my shoulders
Wool hangs loose
He can see my breast
Let him
Want him to
His face changes
Confused
He is spinning and spilling with feelings
Which one
Will come

Sips again from his glass
Tries not to look

She's stronger than you think
Most women are

I take his hand
Lift the finger wearing his wedding band
Place it on my collarbone
Trace it

And besides
She has you

He pulls his hand away
Doesn't know where to look
What to do

I smile
Drink my beer
Glitter at him
His touch still going through me

Is this a joke?
Did she send you?

I shake my head

Who are you?

Shake my head

What's your name?

Shake my head

No? You don't have a name
No? You won't tell me your name

Nola

Nola

I nod
What's your name?

Charlie

Charlie. Hello.

Hi. He shakes my hand
I don't let go

Who are you waiting for, Nola?

No one, I guess
I guess I'm waiting for you

But I'm waiting for my wife

But she's not coming, is she?
Tilt my head towards the empty glasses
Tilt my head towards the empty street

He shakes his head
He laughs but
He looks sad
He finishes his beer

I should go, good to meet you, Nola

We shake hands
Slowly
Fingers interlace
Slowly
Length of my lashes
Softness of them
Brush my cheeks
As I look up at him from under them
He smiles
Bit wonky
He licks his lips

He says, I think I'm a bit drunk
You look like you have stars sparkling in your eyes

He shuts his
Leans back against the ledge and I fall gently
against him
He laughs
Slow and gentle
Puts his hands on my shoulders to steady himself
Opens his eyes
Looks down
Traces my collarbone with his fingers
My nipples harden

Feels them through his shirt

What is happening?

I shrug I smile I close my eyes move my face close
to his
Lips touch
Mine are soft
His are wet
Who are you?

I'm Nola

First kiss
Part my lips
Little tongue
Tastes sweet
And sour
Like beer
Like flesh
Like all the good things in the world I haven't
tasted yet

Mouth moves round to my neck
My ear
Not here

Takes me by the hand
We go down
Steps

He is unsteady
Leads me into a toilet cubicle
First fuck
Fumbling hands
Kissing
He pulls off the dress
Nothing underneath
Raises his eyebrows
Grins
Gets his mouth around my breast
Sucks my nipple whilst unzipping his jeans
Grabs my hand and pushes it against his
expanding flesh
Feel of the cotton
Warmth of his bulge
I want to see it with my eyes
Crouch down on my bouncy new knees
Run my fingers along the veins of his shaft
Touch of the tip is silk
I lick it
Salt and soap
He moans
I am hungry
He lifts my head
Looks into my eyes
Thrusts inside
I am on fire
Spine meets wall

Unkinking the linking discs
Unfurl
Then curl my legs around him
He lifts me
Pushes me higher
I hold on
By the hair
Fingers raking
Taking clumps
Thrust
Flesh
In his mouth
Much of me
To consume
He finds room to plunge deeper
Sends electric
I spark
He splatters
Groans
Wet on the wall
I slide down
Look in his eyes
But he won't look back
Says sorry
To who
Turns around
Throws up in the toilet
I leave

Him sobbing
Him sopping
Stalking up the stairs
I stop to see a stream of red
Rolling down my inner thigh
I leak
I eke
I live.

asleep, dreaming and smiling

I feel around my mouth with my tongue, skin on the inside of my cheeks has come up dry and lumpy like carpet.

I am naked. I feel around my old flesh. Puckered scar. Puncture holes. Skin and bones. I touch between my legs. No trace.

But I am naked. I don't sleep naked. My pyjamas are folded and underneath my pillow. I reach across for Charlie but don't find him there. His side of the bed is cold and empty. Sometimes he sleeps on the sofa, if I'm having a bad night. I get out of bed and put on my dressing gown.

Charlie?

He's not in the living room. Sofa cushions are plush and plumped, unslept on.

It's early. Sunlight is watery. I drink a big glass of water, pour more in the pot to make coffee. My bag and coat is here but not my clothes or shoes. I check my phone.

Voicemail from Sally at 01:47.

Hi babe, your husband is throwing up in my front garden. He told me not to phone you but I didn't want you to be worried... If he ever stops upchucking, I'll bring him inside to sleep on my sofa tonight... Good for nothing! Did I ever tell you you could do better? Hope you are OK... Hope you are feeling better... I'll call you in the morning.

Even though it's freezing outside, I choose to drink my coffee on the balcony. I watch the hot wisps come off the surface of the liquid. My feet are grey as paving stones. The trees in the garden are puny, skinless bones clawing at the sky for something, starving. I let the breeze blow through me. Before I can decide how I'm feeling, Charlie comes home with a bunch of daffodils that haven't bloomed yet. They have yellowing dry leaves that look as sorry as he does. I come inside but leave the doors open. He is shivering. He smells like a packet of cigarettes in a puddle of piss. I take the flowers from him and fill a vase with water before I fill a glass for him. He takes it from me with a shaking hand. I leave him standing there, trying to sip. I have a hot shower, run the water really hot over my feet to see the skin turn red and blotchy.

So much steam, I can't see my face in the mirror, but I decide I am smiling.

in the last months of the year

Couldn't think of anything worse, but Lara said what are you going to do instead? Sit in your room? Watch Jools Holland on your own like a total fucking loser? Nope, not having it, stop moping, get dressed.

She started pulling dresses off hangers and throwing them at me.

Stop! Fine! I'll come! But I'm not wearing a dress, I'm not shaving my legs.

She climbed on the bed and rolled the legs of my pyjamas up.

Bloody hell, Rosy!

She ran her hand up my hairy leg.

I could plait this!

I gave her a little kick.

Who cares? It's not like anyone will see my legs, not like I'll be going home with anyone.

You're coming home with me and I'm not sleeping next to a hairy beast! Go and have a shower, go and sort your life out. I'll get some beers. We're leaving in an hour.

I was annoyed at first. I stood under the hot shower. I didn't want to go to a party full of people I didn't know, I'm no good in big groups. I rubbed my legs with a bar of soap. They weren't that bad. Then I saw a little soapy curl. Jesus. OK. I searched for the pot of body scrub that I knew was there somewhere but hadn't been used for months, put my hand on the lid, which had turned pinky-orange and slimy from sitting water and limescale. I dipped my fingers into the grainy mixture and slathered it over my legs, scrubbed and rubbed in circular motions, took the top layer of dead cells off. I shaved with a sharp new blade. When I had sloughed off my miserable scales I felt better. Conditioned my hair. Lara was drinking cold beer from a bottle, painting her nails bright red when I came out of the bathroom.

Better? she asked.

A bit, I said, taking a swig of beer from the bottle she brought for me. I shaved my legs but I'm still not putting on a dress.

OK, OK, whatever you want. She blew on her nails. Want me to paint yours?

I sat on the bed next to her and spread my fingers. Her brushstrokes were delicate and careful. I watched her face as she concentrated.

They'll need a second coat.

She screwed the lid on the bottle and put it down on the

bedside table.

Shall we put some music on?

She had been slowly coaxing me out of my loneliness. She had become a good friend. But I didn't even know her middle name, her birthday.

What's your middle name?

What?

Your middle name?

Oh, Margaret. Why?

Favourite biscuit?

Custard creams.

Get out of my house! I tossed a pillow at her, laughing. Nobody likes custard creams. What is wrong with you?

Custard creams are harmless, she said. Why all the questions?

I shrugged.

I met Lara when she was crying in the gym over a cheating boyfriend. We went for a coffee and she told me all about it and we got tangled up like old chains in a jewellery box.

You're so weird, she said, smiling.

We linked arms on the walk to the party. She told me who was going to be there, who was cute, who fucked who, who I might like.

Felt like fresh meat. Some guy named Gary kept offering to get me beers, laughed at everything I said, which was very little because he didn't ask me any questions. He put his arm around my waist at one point and I thought he was all right looking but I felt uncomfortable when his hand crept towards my ass, and when he introduced me to someone as 'Josie' I said I was going to find the loo. Someone walked in on me peeing and I think it was Gary, so I held the door shut with my foot.

I went and found Lara and told her I was thinking of going home but she grabbed my hand and said no, no stay!

She made me do a shot of tequila with her.

Stay. Look, there are loads of people here. And I think we'll go to the pub in a minute anyway.

She wouldn't let go of my hand. She introduced me to more people.

Hello.

Hey.

Where do you live?

Yeah, yeah, I know where you mean.

What do you do for a living?

Oh, that sounds interesting.

Wow, working with kids, I couldn't do it, must be really rewarding though.

Any New Year's resolutions?

The usual.

Yep, same.

Same.

Same.

Same.

Coldness of the night air was a relief to me, cooled my burning cheeks but hit Lara like a brick. I rubbed her back as she threw up in a bush. When she was finished she wiped her mouth, reapplied her lipstick and said pub? like nothing had happened.

Are you sure? We can just get a taxi back to mine if you want?

Come on, Rosy! We're going to party! I'm just going to have a big glass of water and then we're going to dance!

We ran to catch up with the crowd. Some guy named James put an arm around Lara and walked her to the bar. She turned her head to wink at me.

We danced.

Oooh! Oooh! Charlie is here!

She twirled me into this poor guy who was standing awkwardly with a pint next to another guy; they were trying to talk but the music was too loud. I nearly knocked the pint out of his hand as Lara shoved me towards him.

Charlie!

She kissed him sloppily on the cheek.

This is my friend Rosy.

She plonked me in front of him and danced away, grinning and winking, shuffling backwards.

We met laughing. His smile was nice.

Hello.

Hey.

You're friends with Lara?

Kind of, I've met her twice, he said.

She is memorable though.

She is.

How do you know her?

We met at the gym. We bonded over how badly we've been treated by men in the past.

Ah, so, I'm actually good friends with her ex.

Shit. Sorry, I didn't know. I mean, I've never met him before. I'm sure he's a good guy deep down and everything, I just think he treated Lara pretty badly. Everyone is good deep down, right?

He smiled and pushed his glasses up onto the bridge of his nose. I liked that I had to bring my head up to look at him and talk to him. He had to lean down to talk to me.

I'm not sure he is a good guy deep down, he said. I don't like what he did to Lara. We stopped speaking for a while because of it. He's getting his shit together now though.

Good, I'm glad to hear that.

I took a sip of my beer.

So, what do you do? he asked.

Disappointing. I was hoping for a little more originality than that. I remember feeling the urge to walk away. But I didn't want to be rude, so I said:

Guess.

OK, he smiled. Well, you look quite young, are you still at uni?

I spluttered, beer nearly fizzed out of my nose.

Um, no, but I'm flattered. I'm a primary school teacher.

Cool!

What about you?

Guess.

OK.

I stepped back to look at him, framed him playfully with my fingers, starting from the top: thick, ruffled, dark-blond hair, acetate glasses, shirt with a jumper over it — navy, but hard to tell in the dark — chinos, one hand in his pocket, electric-blue sneakers. Kind of nerdy, kind of cool.

Gosh, I don't know, you work in... radio?

He smiled widely.

Did Lara already tell you?

No! Am I right?

Yes! Haha! How can you tell?

I don't know, I think maybe it's the shoes?

He looked down at his feet and chuckled.

Yeah, maybe.

What do you do in radio? Are you on the air?

Yeah, he said, blushing hard. I'm a newsreader.

That's cool, I've never met a newsreader before. That sounds exciting.

He looked down, ran his hand through his hair. He looked a bit shy, a bit embarrassed. He was cute.

It's not that exciting. Sometimes I have to do the traffic.

We stood at the bar and talked and talked.

Just before midnight, Lara came over and dragged us into a circle with everyone for the countdown.

THREE!

TWO!

ONE!

He asked me if it would be OK if he kissed me. I nodded and leaned in and we kissed gently.

The pub chucked us out at around 2 a.m. Lara and James were snogging up against the wall outside.

Babe!

She came up for air to tell me she was going home with

James. I gave her a kiss on the cheek and said of course, text me in the morning.

Charlie was lingering, rubbing his hands to warm up.

Are you going home? he asked.

I probably should...

Do you fancy coming back to mine? For a cup of tea? To warm up. My flat is just around the corner.

Sure, just a cup of tea.

He found me a big white T-shirt and boxer shorts to sleep in. He made me tea and toast. His room was clean and neat, but not too neat. He had a record player and stacks of records. We lay down next to each other and listened to Karen O.

He fell asleep so I nipped to the bathroom. He came out of his bedroom as I was coming back. He leaned against the wall to let me pass and I leaned against him. We kissed, my hands touched his chest, his ribs, his stomach. I pressed against him and felt him go hard. He put his hand in the waistband of my boxer shorts, moved his fingers down but I stopped him there.

He wanted me to stay for breakfast, but I told him I needed to go home. He asked me to go out with him the next day and I said yes. I gave him my phone number. He walked me to the Tube station, held my hand on the way and wouldn't let go when we got there. We kissed goodbye.

I had a load of text messages from Lara:

Well?

Did you stay over?

Did you have sex with him?

OMG you dirty stop-out!

OMG did he mention Sam?
I replied with a winky-face emoji, and then:
Who is Karen O??

Lara was invited to our wedding two years later but she didn't come. She was living in Scotland by then, heard she had a toddler, engaged to some guy called Dave. Haven't seen her in a long time.

ill-contained impatience

He doesn't think I'll go on my own, so he makes an excuse to swap his shift at work.

I'll only be sitting around at home wasting the morning, he says.

I'll only be sitting in a chair, in a clinic, wasting time, fluid streaming into my veins, doing absolutely nothing other than making me feel sick, making me feel like shit, for no reason, no good reason.

It isn't helping anyone.

I may as well waste time with you, he says. He puts his arm around me as I stand at the hob stirring porridge. Not really hungry, but probably the last thing I'll eat for days, and it won't burn on the way back up. I treat myself to a teaspoon of peanut butter on top.

Let's take a taxi, says Charlie.

I shake my head. I'd rather take the Tube. I like the walk to the station.

You sure? It's quite far and you'll need your strength today.

I give in. Whatever. I'm not arguing. Fine, we'll take a taxi.

Great, he says. I'll order a car to come in ten minutes.

There is an envelope addressed to me in the hallway downstairs. I open it in the back of the taxi. It is a bright yellow card with a picture of a woman in bed drawn on the front. The woman has a big purple hat on her head, covered in little tissue paper roses. Inside the card are handprints in all colours, cut out and stuck in pairs to make fluttering finger butterflies, with names written on them in their very best handwriting. But I know which handprint belongs to which child just from the colour, the size, the neatness of the print.

Jess has written on the back:

Dear Mrs Winter,
Get well soon. We miss you!
Love,
Reception Class B xxx

That is the cutest thing I have ever seen, says Charlie. He puts his arm around me and kisses the top of my head.

I put it back in the envelope and slide it gently into my bag, taking care not to bend it.

he drew near

I'm not sure it's a good idea, says Charlie.

What do you mean? She's asked me to look after him for a couple of hours, that's all.

Yes, but you haven't been feeling well, Sally knows that. She shouldn't have asked you.

I'm fine, I say. There is absolutely no difference between her asking me today, or six weeks ago.

Well, six weeks ago you wouldn't have been able to look after him because you would have been in work.

Taking Frank to the park for two hours is very different to looking after thirty kids in a classroom all day. And I'll be going back to work soon.

Which is exactly why I think you should be taking it easy and not running around after a toddler all morning.

He comes up behind me, puts his arms around me, kisses the top of my head, tries to melt me like butter.

I turn around and bury my face in his chest. I feel fine today. I want to get out of the flat.

I'm annoyed at Sally for asking you, he says, still holding me tightly.

Don't be, I'm glad she asked, it'll do me some good to be distracted for a while.

I stand on my tiptoes to look at the clock over his shoulder.

You're going to be late for work, I say. I squeeze him to extract a drop of his musk, rub the tip of my nose on his shirt so the scent stays with me for the day.

Did you just wipe your nose on me?

No, I laugh. Maybe a little. I wipe his shoulder with my hand.

I'm on the news desk all day so I won't be able to text you, but if you need me you can phone and I'll try to pick up between bulletins.

I'll be fine, if I need anything I'll just call Sally.

No, he says, I know you'll be fine with Frank, I mean if *you* need me.

I let him go.

I'll be fine, I say again.

I'll always need him. But he can't really give me what I need.

I fill a glass with water, take my anti-sickness and pain relief tablets, drink it down. Tie my hair up, put on my trainers, put on my jacket. We leave the flat together.

Outside he kisses me.

Have a good day, I say.

Don't take any shit, he says.
From Frank?
From my sister, Rosy.

one of these rambles

Oh, thank God! I didn't think you'd come. Charlie just texted me to say I shouldn't have asked you. Why is he being such a dick?

Because he thinks we're Victorians and that I should be in bed, with my hair – not that I have any – in plaits and rags, the sleeve of my nightdress pulled up, physician bent over me, slitting me open to drain the blood, letting the disease and my impurities pour forth.

She kisses me on the cheek and stands to one side to let me in.

It's fucking carnage in here, she says.

Where's Joe? I ask.

Don't ask.

She takes a big gulp from a mug that has 'World's Best Mum' on it in swirly pink writing. She grimaces.

Urgh, it's cold. Sorry, Rosy, I'd offer to make you a coffee but, to be honest, I really just need you to take Frank out for a few hours. I've got a meeting with my manager in fifteen minutes, and I can't bear her to see my knackered fucking face on the screen again. I need to put some make-up on and change out of this crusty top. Sorry.

Of course. Don't worry about it, I'll take him, it's not raining, we can just go to the park. But, um, where is he?

Shit! Frank!

She hands me the mug as she rushes past me into the living room. She comes back with Frank on her hip, hands him to me, takes the mug back.

Hi buddy, I say. He immediately starts screaming. OK, OK, *shhh*, shhh. I start to sway with him, try to soothe him.

Sorry, sorry, OK, Mummy's late, be good for Aunty Rosy. She kisses him on the forehead.

I feel terrible leaving him, she says, going up the stairs.

Don't worry, I say. Come on, Frank, let's go to the park.

He screams louder as I strap him into the buggy. His little arms and legs punch and kick the air. I try to put his shoes on, but he won't keep still, and I'm scared his flailing ankles will snap so I throw a blanket over him and wheel him out of the house. He cries until we get to the end of the street but then I slow the buggy down and crouch beside him and say, look! There's a big red bus! His little mouth opens in wonder and he lets me blow his nose.

We're waiting for the green man, I say and point up to the lights at the crossing. Frank's little finger points too. He says, *ooh!* when the green man lights up.

We pass a steady stream of parents with their kids on their way to school. Frantic, tugging at arms and lunch bags – quick – we'll be late!

I glance at my watch.

It's that time, Frank, everyone is going to school. It'll be you soon. I wonder if you'll come here.

We pause on the corner and look up at the red-brick building. It looks just like my school. I squint in the morning light, shade my eyes to look through the fence to see the little ones. Some running, arms waving, some speeding in on scooters, some holding hands with their parents, reluctant to let go. There are two teachers in the yard to welcome them, smiling, saying good morning to each child, taking hands and bags. I watch a little girl with her mother, the girl has bright red hair and a shy smile, she's holding a bunch of flowers in one hand. Her mother leads her gently towards one of the teachers. She tugs the teacher's coat and holds out the flowers. I look away before the teacher bends down, takes the flowers and folds her into a hug.

My heart aches.

Maybe I'll ask Dr Carson about going back to work, just a couple of days, a couple of hours, even. They grow so quickly, they'll forget me, they'll give their flowers to someone else.

We carry on up the street, wheels rolling smoothly over the pavement. Soon the weight in the buggy changes, I lean over to see Frank lying back, head lolled to the side, sleep sweetly warming his cheeks. I gently tuck his arms under the blanket. I take a photo on my phone and send it to Sally. She replies *Little Fucking Angel*, which makes me smile.

I look up at the houses as we roll by. A neat little row with walled gardens, flowers beginning to bloom. Hums from behind the front doors, letter boxes opening, squeaky swing, metallic clatter, parcels and letters landing on doormats. Babies crying, dogs barking, radio fading under the sound of drilling. Silhouettes in front-door frosted glass, arms pulling on jackets, bags swinging over shoulders, coming, going. Clicks of kettles, whistles, water pouring for tea and coffee. Sounds of lives so different to mine. We have lived suspended in the silence of my sickness for so long. What did we sound like before? What would we sound like if I wasn't sick? Would we buzz? Could you feel us? Would there be a baby?

The questions follow us down the street. We reach the park and enter through a little gate. The path we take is lined with trees; we step into green. Smells wet and fresh. Clumps of cut grass stick to our wheels.

Shall we stop for a coffee, Frank?

He's still fast asleep. He misses ducks in the pond, swans guarding their fluffy silver cygnets. We go by the swings, babies flying high in bumper seats. I'd love to push him on the swings, but sleep seems so necessary, and his cry has the power to wrench the metal chains from the frame. I sit on a bench and rock the buggy back and forth, watching the mothers and fathers and minders. There is a handsome dad with a little boy who looks a little older than Frank. The kid is in the swing and the father is leaning against the metal frame. He is chatting to a woman pushing her child in the other swing. He casually thrusts his arm out every time his little boy's legs kick out towards him. He runs his other hand through his hair now and again. The woman laughs and flicks her hair over her shoulder. I wonder if they know how they look. I wonder when they went from talking to flirting, whether they just met, whether Handsome Dad will notice his kid isn't kicking to go higher but is terrified and twisting in the swing, trying and failing to make it stop. The woman doesn't notice either, they chat and fluff up their hair like chickens about to mate. Makes me feel queasy.

Come on, Frank, let's go.

Charlie would be a handsome dad. I can see him at the school gates, sunglasses on, waving to our little sprout saying *have a great day, honey!* Waiting for them to go in then turning to the mothers, saying, *coffee, anyone?* Strolling, laughing, lapping up the attention. Whilst I'm at work. Teaching other people's kids. The thoughts are bumped out of me by the wheels of the buggy colliding with concrete. Oh.

Do you need a hand?

It is the handsome dad. He gestures to the front of the buggy and the steps I have ploughed into.

Um, yes please, I say, face colouring with embarrassment.

I am dazzled by the grin, the hair, the bulge of his bicep as he pulls the buggy up the steps with one arm, carrying his toddler in the other.

Thank you, I say as he gently sets down the buggy. I thought there was a ramp here.

Oh, there is, it's around the other side though, it's not obvious, he points towards some bushes.

Cute baby, he says. He's still fast asleep.

Thanks, I say.

He lingers. I don't know what for.

I say bye, he smiles and says bye.

No, I don't think Charlie would be like that. I'm being jealous and unfair. Charlie is just friendly and this guy, he's either slimy or lonely. Maybe both.

We wander up to the cafe, a little circular shed with a hatch. I order a coffee and wait by the window. There is a wafting smell of sizzling bacon, and it makes my stomach grumble so I order a bacon sandwich with brown sauce. I sit down at one of the metal tables and take a big bite. The butter has melted softly into the bread. The coffee is scalding hot and takes the top layer off my tongue. But I don't care. Sunlight bounces off puddles, birds tweet and fly and shit. I get some brown sauce on my jeans.

much exercised and nourished

People on wheels
>Trying hard
>Sweating and panting
>Already
>Pumping music
>Flashing lights
>Booming voice from the front

You're too late!
The class has started already!
You'll have to wait for the next one!

Walk to the front
Look at this guy in the silver leggings

I don't think so.

Straddle a bike in the front row
Woman next to me slows her spin
Gives a real dirty look
Good
Look at me
Bitch

Can't take his eyes off me
Lean forward and smile

Let's take it up a notch, you're not here for a pleasant Sunday ride, you're here to WORK! My resistance is fourteen, RPM sixty, I am working to eighty per cent of my capacity. LET ME SEE YOURS!

Fourteen
Sixty
Easy
He's watching me
Watch back
Eyes
Eyes
Smile

Blood flowing through me
Fast and thick

Take my hands off the handlebar
Run my finger under the band of my sports bra
No sweat
No sticking
Lift my loose hair
Twist it on top of my head
Touch my elegant neck

Rise when they rise
Yawn
Stretch
Feels good
Land back on the seat
Perfect pear shape
Pressing against my perfect
Pussy
Grind
Buck my hips
Ride
Ride
Ride

If you can give a bit more, give it now, increase the resistance!

Woman next to me turns her dial the other way
Red-faced
Puffing
Slowing

I speed up
Match pace
Rolling with the silver legs
Those thighs
I'd like to sit on his lap

Keep going!

He gets off his bike to walk around the class
Feel his eyes on me from behind
Breath on my neck

Wow, you're doing great, but careful you don't overdo it
I look back at him and laugh
And laugh
And laugh
Legs spinning
I rise
And rise
Red-faced woman opens her mouth
In awe of my ascent
Spinning stops
They all watch
Me float through the ceiling.

might indeed be possible to cover my face

The first one I watch is half an hour long. I count the pieces of make-up and tools as the video runs. Sixteen. Sixteen! And she says the words sculpting, baking, blending, highlighting, like I'm supposed to know what they mean. I know what they mean, but I don't know what they have to do with my face.

She's young at the start of the video. She has a sprinkling of spots on her chin but in a pretty way. Oil on her face is her chemistry changing. It is pain, excitement, a flood of miracles that dries up too soon. I want to tell her she doesn't need to cover her spots but she'd be mortified the way I was. Make-up was shit when I was her age. Clumping, orange, more distracting than concealing, not worth bothering with in the end. I watch her streak and shape and buff. The result is interesting and terrifying. Who is she now? Unrecognisable in thirty minutes. Could commit crimes with this face and never get caught. She is older, inquisitive, with fixed arched eyebrows, alluring with eyelines and lashes that flick. And lips. What will she do with those? I pause the video when her head is tilted to one side, cheeks drawn in, lips slightly puckered. I don't know why but I feel sick. I am looking at a clown and it makes me feel sad.

Do a shoulder shake, take a sip of water, type *make-up tutorial for chemo patients* in the search bar and all the little squares fill up with bald heads and big smiles. I take *The Empress* out of her envelope and tuck her into the mirror frame. I look at her. She looks at me. I look at myself in the mirror. The sight of the size and shape of my hairless head still shocks me. I feel like someone is standing behind me, always, holding a single pale-pink helium balloon on a string. But I don't feel so alone any more. I didn't think there would be so many of them, so many of us.

I look back at the screen and scroll. I'm looking for a woman around my age but then I realise we are all ageless babies, no grey giveaways, wrinkled for a different reason. I choose a recent video with 30K views, titled *Everyday Make-up Tutorial for Chemo Patients*. The woman is called Erin and I like her face because it is neutral. Her bio is short, matter-of-fact, no pity, no warriors here, just carrying on. I keep my eyes up, hide the comments, watch the video. I follow along, drawing discreet eyebrows and feeling immediately better. Cheeks a little too pink, but by the end I see someone else in the mirror, someone I don't mind the look of, someone I don't feel pity for. I don't look like who I was before, but I'm not who I was before, so it doesn't matter. Maybe if you looked really closely you would see I'm sick, but at a glance, walking down the street, sitting across from me on the bus, I think I'd have you fooled. I take the wig out of the bag. I haven't worn it yet, haven't even tried it on. I brush it out, run my fingers through it, the hair feels thick and glossy, too glossy. Long and straight, like my hair was, sandy-blonde in the summer. I tip my head forward and pull it on, tip my head back and let the hair fall around my shoulders. I pull it up off my forehead a little bit and untuck my ears. I take a selfie and send it to Charlie. He replies straight away with a love-heart emoji. I send one back. He replies *Let's go out tonight* and I feel a flutter in my stomach. I sit for a few minutes and look at myself in the mirror. I say to myself, it's not about vanity, it's about confidence. I say thank you, Erin, and click to close the page.

never heard of him

I arrive in a white room full of eyeballs in the heads of people
who have never seen anyone like me before
>But I like it
>All eyes staring at me
>In silk
>Burnt-orange slip
>Wasn't going to buy it
>Spaghetti straps
>Low crescent cut at the back
>Long
>Skims my shins
>Shimmers when I walk
>Someone says picks out the golden tone of my hair
>Someone says how can she walk in those shoes

Had to practise
Picking my way along the pavement on two pins
Now I'm towering
Toned
I turn away from the eyes
Take a glass of champagne
Meant to sip but I've never tasted anything so
Sharp
So
Sparkling
So I take another glass
And walk through the room
Waves of people part
Stand against the only bit of white wall that doesn't have a
painting hanging on it
Burn against the wall in my bright colours

I am approached
Leans against the wall
Turns his head to me
His teeth are shine-and-clink white
Like a ceramic toilet
He likes himself
He's talking about himself
He asks me what brings me here
I point down at my feet
He laughs
Is he OK in the head?

Then I realise so I gesture with a limp wrist to the paintings
Clearly not
He keeps talking
Yawn loudly
Finish my drink
Says he'll fetch me another
No
Insists
Idiot
He leaves

Another arrives
A woman with curls and brown eyes
She likes my dress
She wants to know if I know anyone here
Wrap a curl around my finger
Surprise rises in her eyes
Drop the curl
Put my finger to her lip
Press the juicy flesh
Fingertip stained pink
She leans in to kiss but I say
I'm not here for you
Calls me a teasing bitch
Turns and walks into Idiot with the drinks
Spills
Fizzing fountains
Drenches her dress

Laugh and leave them

He's here somewhere

I stand in front of two big orange canvases
Fat purple thighs and a penis
Blood smear
Or sauce spill
I say is this art?
And he says
What the fuck are you doing here?
Breath on my bare shoulder
Don't turn around
Closer
His cold champagne glass presses against my back
Oh
I reach around
Take it from him
Drink
Doesn't move
His thighs lightly press against mine
Turn around
Watch his face
Anger lifts
Like clouds from the moon
Eyes glint
Like stars
You look

Different

But I'm the same, I say with my lips close to his ear

I disappear
Into the crowd
Find a dark place
Shadows
Spotlights turned to illuminate a massive piece
A masterpiece, someone says
An indigo man sitting in a chair
Screaming
Can't tear their eyes away
So won't see me
Standing in the corner
Waiting

He finds me soon enough
He brings more champagne
I don't take it from him
He says

Nola
Your name is not on the guest list

It's not

Then why are you here?

I came to see something beautiful

I turn my head to the painting

Why are you here, Charlie?

I'm here for work

I look at the glasses of champagne in his hands

And what is it that you do?

He's turning red

I'm a journalist

I nod

And why are you here, Charlie?

Looking in his eyes
Won't break his gaze
He's looking back
I touch his cheek
Skin is smooth
Shaved to look sharp
Clean white pressed collar
Move my hand to his neck

His lips part to say
Nothing

Tips of our noses touch
Mouths are open
Pressed against
Crushing the silk of my dress
Hard and trembling
He holds a glass to my lips
I sip
A drop spills
Rolls down my chin
Down my neck
Running like a raindrop
I pull the strap off my shoulder
Dress slips off
My breast
Bare
Show him my perfection
Bends his head
Licks the drop of champagne
Gentle tongue traces
Lips brush
Suck my puckered nipple
I gasp
I say

What about your wife?

Stops
Head straight
Teeth clenched

What do you know about my wife?

I know she can't fuck you any more

Fuck off, he spits

He walks away

I wave goodbye.

the appearance of a friend

When I see Megan in the bay I start crying. She hugs me. There, there, she says.

Charlie is behind me, he says quietly: she's finding it tough at the moment.

I turn my head and shoot him a look. Did he think I wouldn't hear him? Does he have any idea what he's saying?

Megan gives me a squeeze and then releases. I don't want her to.

She searches my face. Tells me I look tired.

Charlie, would you mind grabbing us a coffee please, I say.

He is surprised but delighted to be useful.

Of course. Megan, it's a skinny latte, right?

Well remembered, yes please, she says.

I'll have my usual please, I say.

Of course, darling.

He pecks me on the cheek and leaves.

I feel like he's holding a plastic bag over my head. I can't move, I can't breathe. He wants to control everything. We sink into our chairs.

I hate to say it, she says, but at least he's here.

But I don't want him here.

You don't mean that, she says.

Maybe I don't.

My husband left me when I told him I had cancer, she says. She runs her hands over the salty blonde stubble on her head.

Are you serious?

She nods slowly.

Yup. Said it was too much for him, wouldn't be able to cope. Hates hospitals, wouldn't be able to come with me to any of my appointments, he said I deserved someone who could look after me properly and I agreed with him.

That really takes the biscuit, I say. I reach out for her hand.

It really bloody does. You're entitled to feel how you feel, Rosy, it is your cancer at the end of the day. But doing this on your own is hard. I'm better off without my waste-of-space husband for sure, but I'm really lonely.

I'm sorry, I say. I feel ungrateful now. I just wish he'd let me cope with things in my own way, instead of assuming he knows what any of this feels like for me.

She nods. She knows.

Did you hear about Audrey? she asks.

Yes. I don't know how to tell Charlie.

hearty, healthy, dapper, red-faced

Your lipstick matches the chairs, he says, lips brushing my ear. It does. This place is incredible.

Warmly lit and everything is pink.

It kind of looks like a vagina, I whisper, then my face colours as I realise the hostess is standing right behind me, waiting to take my coat.

Isn't it fabulous? she says, smiling.

It is fabulous.

She goes to lift the coat from my shoulders, but Charlie stops her, steps in, says thanks but I'll do that. She doesn't drop her smile, but she raises her eyebrows slightly.

Of course, sir.

She takes a little step away from me.

He eases my arm out of my coat like he's taking a soufflé out of the oven. The hostess is watching curiously, to see if it collapses, watching a cigarette burning to the end, no one breathes until the cylinder of ash falls. But it doesn't. It's just my arm, normal arm, in a sheer black sleeve. Hostess looks puzzled. Charlie hands her my coat. I am thoroughly embarrassed. Charlie looks at me and says, what?

You don't need to do that any more, I'm fine now, completely fine. That's why we're here.

I'm your husband, Rosy, I'll always help you out of your coat.

He sounds a bit annoyed. I take his hand and kiss it and say thank you.

There they are.

Sally waves wildly from a table in the corner. Joe is on his phone. He doesn't look up until I try to pull back the chair next to him, gosh, it's heavier than it looks, Charlie nearly falls over to reach it and stop me trying to lift it. I'll do that, he says, then Joe looks up from his phone.

God, sorry Rosy, let me get that for you. He pushes the chair back and leans in to give me a quick peck. Shakes hands with Charlie.

Sally has trouble shuffling out of the booth.

These chairs are like quicksand, she says, getting to her feet to wrap me in a hug. You look amazing, she says. Gorgeous. Like a pixie, like Mia Farrow in *Rosemary's Baby* ...you know, when she's still chic. She kisses her brother on the cheek. You look all right too, she says, shirt and tie! Joe didn't feel like it, she says quietly to me, rolling her eyes.

We sink into the plush pink velvet chairs. I stroke the fabric.

This place is amazing. It's so PINK, I say, looking up at the walls, different layers and textures of pink and gold, glimmering.

Joe pipes up, oh yeah it's completely OTT but the food is actually pretty good. I came with a client a few weeks ago.

Oooh, very fancy, I say. I think I'd like to work in publishing.

That's what everyone says, but people don't realise, it's actually really hard work. These client lunches are work, you've always got to be ON, he says and takes a sip of sparkling water.

Oh, of course, I'm sure it is hard work. I just meant it must be nice having lunch in a fancy restaurant from time to time, instead of leftovers in the staffroom.

Charlie gives me a look, maybe I sound defensive. Joe is about to say something else. I have a feeling it's something like *you chose to be a teacher* but Sally cuts in with:

Right, what's everyone drinking? Shall we start with some fizz?

Joe does a quiet cough.

Oh and tonight is on us, by the way, we're celebrating, so order whatever you want! says Sally with a wink.

Joe looks furious. Charlie looks furious. I look down at the menu.

No, no we can't let you do that, it's very generous of you, but we can't let you do that, I say.

Charlie says, absolutely not, no way! We asked you to come out with us, we're paying.

Then Joe says, no, really we'll get this, you guys have had a shit year and Rosy hasn't really been working much, you know, it can't have been easy, you know, financially, on top of everything else.

Oh God. He *actually* said that. I'm already sunken in the

chair but if I could sink further, I would. There is smoke coming out of Charlie's ears. I can feel his body tense, fists clench under the table.

Thanks, mate, but we're all right actually. I've picked up a ton of new voice work and Rosy's going back after the summer.

I nod.

Sally grimaces.

Bottle of champagne arrives. We sit in silence as it's poured.

Sorry, I didn't mean anything by it, says Joe.

Let's toast! says Sally. Let's celebrate! She raises her glass. To Rosy, she says.

To health, says Joe.

To my beautiful wife, says Charlie.

To the worst year of my life behind me, I say. And to you guys.

We clink the paper-thin flutes together.

So, what would you recommend, Joe? Everything on the menu looks delicious.

mauled the unresisting body

Bubbles up quickly, out of nowhere, like a blister on your heel after an hour in bad shoes. I am simmering in my sweat when he wakes me up.

Rosy, are you OK? You're soaking, the sheets are drenched. What?

My vision is blurry, the room is on fire. Is this a migraine?

I don't feel well, I say, turning over on my side. I'm going to be sick.

He's on his knees by my side of the bed. He puts an ice-cold wet flannel on my forehead and a bucket by the bed. The smell of the bucket makes me heave, the bucket that we keep our cleaning products in, it smells like bleach and vinegar and puke. Acid rises, stomach clenches, the outpouring is orange, clogs my nostrils.

He rubs my back.

It's OK, he says, get it all up.

I start to cry.

It's OK, he says, *shhh, shhh*.

I blow my nose, it burns, I shudder. I spit into the bucket.

Better? he says.

I shake my head.

What's wrong?

The moment is a bad memory, we've been here so many times before. Charlie on his knees by my side, me hurling my guts up into a container. Unwelcome echo, rolling around the room, flattening us.

I can't crush him, so I lie.

Must be a bug, I say. I feel like shit.

We should go to hospital, he says, you need to be seen.

No, no, we shouldn't go anywhere near a hospital if I've got a virus, they'll turn us away anyway. I just need to rest, it'll run its course. You should probably keep away too, I don't want to make you ill.

No way, I'm staying right here.

He sits on the floor, back against the bed with his arms folded.

You might want to move over a little bit...

I vomit again. The sound is worse the second time round. He reaches up for my hand, our fingers entwine. I lie back onto the damp pillow, it feels cool for a moment.

I'd better open some windows, he says.

I rigour through the night, the next day, the day after. I don't know how long I'm in bed for, I can't see through the fits of fever and fatigue. Charlie changes my pyjamas, holds a glass to my lips, but I'm dog-sick and I can't drink. I hear him talking.

Who is here?

He doesn't answer me.

Can't turn on my left side. Pain is excruciating. Yellow stain on my sleeve. Is it sweat? Is it sick?

Man in my room. Can't make out his face, but it isn't Charlie, so I start screaming.

Rosy! Rosy! It's OK, shhh, shhh, calm down, I'm here. We need to go to hospital now, this is Raj and Billy, they're going to help us get you down the stairs and into the ambulance.

I scream louder.

Charlie says, I'll carry her, maybe that'll be easier.

He scoops me up like a baby.

It'll be all right, he says soothingly into my ear. He kisses me on the cheek. I let him take me because what else can I do?

chief of sufferers

I listen for him.

I hear his footsteps tread to the front door but he doesn't open it. He walks through the hallway back towards our room. He opens the door quietly, bright sunlight startles him.

You're up? he says.

I'm sitting up in bed. I smile at him weakly.

It's freezing in here! You'll catch your—

It's OK, Charlie, leave the windows open please. I'm not cold, I like the fresh air.

He has rushed in and closed them all before I've finished speaking.

He turns and starts to say something, but his lips are stopped by the smell. He tries, he tries really hard, but he can't stop the disgust rippling over his face, lips parting, teeth showing.

I sigh, because the pity and the pleading come next. He squeezes onto the bed next to me. Takes both of my hands.

Please. Please. I'm begging you.

He has tears in his eyes.

He has never cried, not once, the whole way through. If he had cried, if he had listened, maybe things would be different.

I shake my head. I can't speak. Can't articulate the pain.

He buries his face in the bedclothes. I don't run my fingers through his hair.

I just want you to stay, he says.

I will stay, I say.

His face is red and wet and angry when he looks up at me.

How? How can you when you won't even try! You won't even try the treatment!

LOOK AT ME! I howl from the embers of the last lit fire low in my gut. I have had the treatment! There is nothing more. There is nothing left.

Chemo! The doctor said you can have more chemo!

Charlie, I can have palliative chemo, symptom relief, that's it.

Then have it. Please. Give us more time.

More time for what? More time to have sickness and diarrhoea, to lie sleeplessly in this room. For what?

His hands grip me so tightly, there is so little left he could squeeze the life out of me here and now.

Come with me to see Jacqui, I say.

You've lost your fucking mind, he says. No. You're not going to see any more nutters. Over my dead body.

My shoulders shake with silent laughter until I can't hold it in any longer and I laugh and laugh and laugh in his face.

not fitting language

My mother asks about Frank. She's hungry for his baby smell and skin. She met him once when he was newborn. She is desperate to be a grandmother. I show her some photos on my phone Sally sent me. Up to his eyeballs in ice cream, toddling around the garden in a hat too big for him. There's one of the three of them, Frank on Sally's lap, Joe with his arms around them. Frank is looking in the wrong direction and has a funny little sly smile on his face like he's plotting something or breaking wind. Sally has her eyes shut, mouth is heart-shaped smiling, she's probably swearing. Joe is smiling too, his fingers are clenched around them both, he's holding on, looking right at the camera. He looks normal. Not at all like an asshole. I'm looking for clues but I don't want to pull the smile off his face and I don't see anything but a happy family, captured in bliss, a moment to die for. The photo was taken just a couple of weeks ago.

You shouldn't get involved.

I'm not, Mam. It's just difficult when Sally texts me or rings and asks me to look after the baby. What am I supposed to say? No?

What does Charlie think?

What do you mean, what does he think? I don't know. I don't think Sally has really talked to him about it. And what does it matter what he thinks, Sally's my friend too and Frank is my nephew!

I know, darling, I just think it's a shame people can't get along, for the baby's sake at least.

This isn't people not getting along, this is a man who is not pulling his weight and a woman who is fed up of it.

Don't be unfair, he's working, isn't he?

What do you think Sally does all day?

I don't know... it was different in my day.

It isn't any different now. It's just the same, that's the point, that's the problem. But there's no point, it's not her fault and it's not worth fighting over.

I shuffle my bum forward to get off the sofa. I'm irritated.

Where do you think you're going?

She hands me back my phone and pushes me gently into the cushions.

I was just going to make a cup of tea!

I'll do that, you sit there. You're meant to be taking it easy.

Mother, making us a cup of tea isn't exactly back-breaking work – please just let me do it.

But she's already up, shuffling off to the kitchen, I can hear her opening every cupboard and every drawer looking for cups and spoons even though she's been here so many times before.

He's cute though, that baby, she shouts. You can just tell he's full of mischief! It's nice that you're spending a bit more time with him. I bet it makes you feel broody.

Not really. You forget I spend all day with children and it's nice at the end of the day when they go back to where they came from.

She comes back into the room with tea in mugs that I don't like, that I was given as a gift, that I hid in the back of a cupboard, that I had forgotten existed.

I put my hands out to take one from her but she says, no, no, it's too hot, and puts it down on the coffee table.

I've brought biscuits!

She starts rifling through her bag. She's brought her knitting. She pulls out a bright blue ball of wool, hands it to me, pulls out a packet of chocolate digestives and puts them on the coffee table.

What do you think of this? she says, holding up half of a jumper with a red rocket on the front.

It's a bit small for me, I say.

She gives me a poke with a knitting needle.

Not for you! For Frank!

I know, I was joking. Yeah, it's cute. It's very blue.

Well, he is a little boy! I think it will suit him, don't you?

She caresses the soft wool. Her eyes are sad.

It's lovely, I say. I'm sure Sally will like it, she can't knit or anything like that.

I reach for my tea, take a gulp.

Urgh! Is there sugar in this?

Just half a teaspoon! You look like you need it.

It's a small thing, but it makes me want to weep.

Oh, just drink it, it won't harm!

I've knitted one just like it for Wendy's grandson.

She starts knitting.

Who is Wendy?

You know, Wendy. We've started walking together on a Friday. I met her at the car boot sale with your father. She bought some of the little booties I made. We got talking, turns out she lives just up the road from us. I've told you about Wendy. Her grandson is the one with the funny name.

God. I can only imagine.

Rosy!

What?

Since when do you take the Lord's name in vain?

Since the Lord isn't saving me – though of course I don't say this out loud.

I try to drink but I can't. I hold the mug in my icicle hands for warmth.

Her mouth moves to count the stitches, I catch the numbers on her breath as she whispers, her head is slightly dipped, eyes concentrating on her needles. Her face is the same as when she prays. Peace about her. Needles click and clatter. Settle back into the sofa, shut my eyes. Dozing, maybe dreaming, I hear her whispering I hope you can still have children, I hope one day you will. I hope these drugs don't take that away from you.

Maybe she didn't say that, maybe it was in my dream. In my dream there was a ball of blue wool knotting up my organs, squeezing every last drop of blood out of them. They become dry and black and hard like lumps of coal. A big bald baby pulls the thread and they come out in a long line. The big bald baby drags them like a wooden pull-along train.

I wake up to the sound of the kettle boiling. She brings me a fresh cup of tea in the same bad mug but this time without sugar.

She says, shall we watch a bit of telly and have a biscuit?

I say yes.

a hissing intake of the breath

Not meant to be here. Sneaking in, in the dark, carefully closing the door behind me. Making out the shapes. Rows of bikes rise like waves, handles jutting out, sharp shark fins circling a single bike. But look again, they're bowing, surrendering. Weaving between them, tapping the handlebars as I go, I make my way to the front row, the centre bike. Hop on, clip in, face the phantom instructor.

Feet feel like they belong to the pedals, bike is a body part, wheel turns, legs propel as easy as blinking. I can hold on with one hand, I am not held back. Knees soft, feeling the full circle. I rise up, chest proud. In the dark there is no difference in the size of my breasts, there is no lump bulging from my underarm. In the dark the sensations of my sickness sit with me. I acknowledge the ache, the ooze, the itch. But they don't define me here. They are pushed to the peripheries by my big beating heart. Legs ploughing through the hours, turn my hours into days. Muscles pound the flesh squeeze the sweat through the mesh of my skin and if I push it all out, if it sloughs off climbs the ropes of my veins it can get out it can FUCK OFF. I am shrill. The fuck and the off penetrate the heartbeat so loud my brain is bouncing in my skull, sending shards of sweat chipped off the sheen across my forehead, dropping on the rubber floor melting to nothing like snowflakes.

Shimmering with strength. Pulsing with power. In here, I am living forever.

Flash of light. Someone is coming for me. I don't slow down. I won't go.

Glimmer in the mirror.

What's that?

Who's there?

I look up.

White teeth.

She's here. She rises. A goddess.

Single strip of blue light overhead illuminates her. She is naked. Her skin is silver. Hair loose and falling like rain. The whites of her eyes are burning bright metal.

She spins. We synchronise. She says nothing. Doesn't blink. Doesn't breathe.

We spin to the beat of my erratic heart. Where is hers? Her grin is fixed. She hears the question in my head.

I glance to the side to see her in the mirror. I want to see her breasts. But she's not there. I am there, multiplied a hundred times over.

Her eyes haven't moved from me. Her hands come off the handlebars, she balances, legs still spinning she puts her hands to her mouth, she cups a kiss and blows it to me. It is poison but I can't help but breathe it in. She moves her hands over her chest, her fingers rest on her nipples. She bites her lip to show me her pleasure. Then they travel down to her hips, perfectly curved, her stomach perfectly flat. She rubs her hands over her belly, places a fingertip in her navel then slowly rips it open. She peels back her skin to show me her insides.

Her stomach is slimy and black and high up in her ribcage, layers of intestine cushion an expanding amniotic sac filled with foetuses floating around like blue blobs in a lava lamp. Lit up. Hundreds of hands with no fingers wave to me.

Open my mouth to be sick or to scream but nothing comes out.

Her bike begins to roll towards me in slow sadistic motion and I am frantically trying to slow my pace my legs are propelled round and round sweat-drenched hands lose their grip on the handlebars she is closer now closer close enough that I can smell the sweetness of her breath the salt of her serous fluid the iron of her blood. The foetuses float before me mouths open saying Mama little circular mouths like wheels still spinning legs still struggling against the speed I roll eyes roll blacking out. Her hand reaches for me will she save me from falling? Hand pushes past pounds down on the brake wheel halts pedals pause sound of my ankle snapping cracks the mirror.

delighted me like wine

Rosy found him online
    Sent him the selfies I took on her phone
    Set the date, time and place, told him he couldn't reach me
until then
    I don't know why she did it
    Wanted to feel involved
    In control
    So funny
    What's wrong with meeting people in real life
    In the moment
    Walk up to the bar
    With a smile
    Tap someone on the shoulder, say, let's talk, buy me a
drink. Kiss them on the mouth.

Laid out the green dress which, in fairness, is gorgeous
Silk, again, bad for sitting, getting wrinkled
But she just can't get over the fact that I don't leave
sweat stains
Incredible
So the green dress, the strappy shoes
Little much for dinner and drinks
Maybe I can get him to go dancing

I am late
He already has a drink in his hand
A cocktail
Cherry on a stick
I want the cherry
So
I take it
He looks surprised
Bemused
Then he smiles

Nola?

Hi

Do you take cherries from all the strange men you meet?

Are you strange?

I meant strangers

You said strange men

He laughs
He is unsure
I smile at him, chewing

What's that?

I point to his glass

Old Fashioned

I'll have one
Please

Sure, he turns to the bar, orders the drink
Turns back
Puts out his hand for me to shake it

I'm Henry

I know

I shake his hand
Hands are soft
Babyish

Perch on the bar stool next to him
Get close to study
So why him?
Same height as Charlie
Thinner
Unremarkable face
Clean-shaven
Good teeth, little gap between them at the front, want to put the tip of my tongue in it
Smells minty
Expensive clothes
Take a sip
Make a face

You don't like it?

Too sweet

He laughs

OK, we can move on to wine with dinner, if you like?
You look beautiful, by the way

He's trying too hard
But he's right

It's a good dress, isn't it?

I turn to show him the back
Backless
Put my hand over my coccyx
Run it up to feel silk meeting skin
Difference is imperceptible
Can't peel his eyes away
Finishes his drink and pays up
Maybe this is why she picked him
Flash of the little gold card

Shall we?

He wants to put his hand on the small of my back

I hope Italian is OK?

My face is blank

He says again, a little louder, like I didn't hear him, do you
like Italian food?

I've never had Italian food

He laughs, sees my face, says

Seriously?

I smile and shrug my shoulders

Oh, OK, well I think you'll like it, are you hungry?

Starving

Feed me

He takes my arm and we walk out and around the corner
He tells me on the way where he lives, what he does for
a living

PR

What's that?

He laughs, again, he says

Do you know what? I don't really know myself!
You're funny

I'm not trying to be

Maybe not, but I like that you make me laugh

I don't understand why he thinks that is important

We walk into a little restaurant with a red awning
Cosy room
Tablecloths and candles

Busy, buzzing
One table free
People with red cheeks and red lips from red wine
White plates

We are seated by a serious man holding many menus
Bottle of red
Fizzy water
Pages and pages
Henry points to the menu and says

This is good, that's meant to be really nice too, if you
wanted something a bit lighter

Waiter brings big plates heaped with something creamy-
looking to the table next to us

Carbonara
And
Garlic bread

Sets down the plates then turns to us

Are you ready to order?

Henry gestures to me
I shake my head
No, you first

OK, I'll have the calamari please
Then, the puttanesca

Fishy

Some salad?

And for you?

Pen hovering impatiently over tiny notepad
Hovering hand annoys me so I take a sip of my wine first

Nola?

Yes
I'll have the carbonara and garlic bread
Please

Smiling sweetly
Sipping wine
Henry raises an eyebrow

The garlic bread looks massive

His eyes are over on the table next to ours watching a man
eating garlic bread
To share? I'm not a huge fan...

Waiter waits
Like I might change my mind
Waiter says

Yes, madam, it is a large portion

Henry says

I thought we could get some dessert too

Great, yes, dessert too, but don't we order that afterwards?

Waiter says

Very good

Stuffs his notebook in the pocket of his apron
Takes our menus
Bustles off

Bigger sip of wine

Carbs-on-carbs
He grins
Not a nice grin

Don't worry
I'll still fuck you

He turns the colour of the wine
Takes a long time to die out of his cheeks because I won't
look away from him
Fiddles with his knife and fork

So, tell me about you

What do you want to know?

Where are you from?

Where am I from?

Are you going to answer every question I ask with
a question?

I laugh
No, I just don't know how to answer
I don't really know where I'm from

This confuses him
Eyebrows knot
It's honest, at least

Oh, OK
Where are you from, Henry?

Boring, boring, Surrey, blah, blah

He talks until the food comes
Small table suddenly filled with steaming cheesy stringy
Red green acid salt
P A S T Aaah

Would you like black pepper, madam?

Waiter is wielding a long thick wooden bulbous rod
glinting silver knob on the end
Holds it diagonally above me
Waiting for me to say
Yes
I take it from him
His mouth does a little o
It's lighter than it looks
The wood is smooth
Rounded head
Wrap my hand around it
Feel the silver
Cold
Smooth
Twist
Little black grains sprinkle
Twist
Twist
Shower my plate
Flecks in the creamy sauce
Makes me sneeze

Makes me laugh

Do you want some black pepper, Henry?

Angle it over his plate
His face
Confused
Concerned
I smile
Then he
Laughs

Sure!

I grind until he raises his hand
Thanks

Waiter sighs all over us
I hand it back to him
He walks away quickly
Henry is still laughing
He takes my hand
Interlocks our fingers
Says
Where are you from, Nola?

But he's not asking for an answer
We tuck in.

sought with tears and prayers

Ready?

She bites her thin lip and touches my cheek with a cold, wrinkled hand. She searches my eyes but doesn't find what she's looking for.

When we stood here, that moment she touched me on our wedding day, I was brimming with joy and hopefulness. She took my arm and walked me down the aisle and I was floating.

She is searching for something like hope. Breaths are short, pressing back her tears.

I nod and try to smile. She takes my arm but I can barely feel her hand through the layers, vests and jumper and scarf and two coats.

She pushes open the heavy wooden door and leads me into the church. We walk slowly, footsteps sticking to the stone floor, hear them clapping over the mournful organ. Heads turning towards us, my mother nodding solemnly to those clasping their hands in prayer or reaching to touch her arm. No one wants to touch me. When we reach the altar Reverend James takes both her hands and bows his head, says a short prayer I can't hear. Lifts his head, says amen, looks at me, smiles, says hello, Rosy, how are you?

Peachy, I say, smiling back, showing teeth.

My mother pinches me hard, I feel it this time. The look she gives could rip the paper skin right off my face. She pushes me towards a pew.

Sorry, reverend, thank you, she says.

I shuffle sideways into the pew. I glance at the rows of people behind us before I sit. A gasp goes up, a woman covers her open mouth with her hand. I give her a shrug. What am I to do with this face, this body?

Just ignore them, she says. He's glad you're here.

She doesn't mean Reverend James, who won't look in my direction, who seems lost for words, who is holding his bald head in his hands.

She hands me coins for the collection plate like when I was a child. I stack them neatly, careful not to make a sound.

We start with a hymn but I can't stand. I sing along quietly though; I remember the words.

When Reverend James starts his sermon, I struggle to listen, I pick at the old crumbling varnish on the pew with my brittle thumbnail. The glass of water on the lectern catches my eye, the water quivers as the reverend lifts and lowers his hands.

When he had hair, when I was little, he gave a lesson. There was a small table with empty glasses and great jugs of water. He asked for volunteers to come to the front and fill the glasses. He asked: how much does God love us? Fill the glass to show the amount of love and say why. The first water was poured by my mother, to the brim, without spilling, and she said, His love fills us up. The reverend nodded. True, but not correct. My mother was annoyed and sat back down with her arms folded. An elderly lady with a stick took ages to make her way to the front. She handed the stick to the reverend and filled her glass half full. She said if it was more than this I wouldn't be in so much pain. She snatched the stick back and made her way back to her chair. I raised my hand and got called up. I filled the glass an inch from the top, like how I was shown to pour water at the dinner table, I didn't say anything and the reverend said, you're very close, Rosy, but love is not neat and tidy. I sat back down next to my mother's frown. A man got up, he lifted an empty glass, he turned it upside down and slammed it back down on the table. The water wobbled in the jugs, the reverend reached out to the man, then withdrew his hand when he saw his angry face. The man stormed out of the church. The reverend cleared his throat. He turned over the empty glass, took a jug and poured. And poured, and poured. My mother gasped as water flowed to the floor. God's love is endless, said the reverend. It doesn't just fill, it overflows, he said, as the water in the jug ran out.

Yes, yes, says my mother. She said it then, she says it now, whispering.

We are asked to pray, I bow my head and I ask myself: am I

full of love? And I ask God: why am I suffering? He answers by setting my insides on fire, I feel burning from my guts to my glottis, then He says: I will pour water, I will put the fire out. Soon.

Will He save me?
Will He cure me?
Will He kill me?

to the great, dark bed

Whatever he was worried about doesn't worry him any more
    His tongue is in my mouth
    Wall to cheek wall tastes of red wine
    Coffee, maybe, but nothing else remains
    Hands on my waist
    Belly isn't bigger for the meal
    Fingering my hips through the silk

    Will you come in, for a drink?

    He's got me up against the door of a nice house
    Doesn't unlock his lips when he unlocks the door
    Key in with his eyes closed
    Door swings and stumble

Into the dark
Takes his hands off my hips
Claps twice
Lights on
Low
Some kind of slow music
Sexy
Is it?
His kisses slow
He says

I just need to go to the bathroom, I'll get us that drink
Make yourself at home

He gestures to the large sofa
It is so big I could lie down three times on it
I lie down
Curl my legs round the corner
Rub my legs over the velvet
Calves sinking into the cushions
Inky blue room
Smells like a single man
Silver and gold gadgets
Glossy books of girls and cars on the coffee table
Concrete ashtray
Candles with black burnt wicks
He comes back into the room
Hands washed

Runs them over the smooth countertop
Looks like marble
Might be
Takes two crystal glasses out of the cabinet
Pours amber liquid
Large measures
He takes a gulp
Tops it up
Brings it over
Sets down on cork coasters
Lifts my legs
Sits
Lowers them into his lap
He feels them
Fingers tracing towards my thighs
Up
Then
Down
To my ankles
Will he unstrap my shoes?
He doesn't
Fingers rest on my knees
Reaches for his drink
Sinks back into the sofa
Closes his eyes
Drifts
Drinks
Drifts

Dig my heel into his thigh

Hey! What was that for?

You're sleeping?

No, no, I'm resting my eyes

He rubs his belly

All that food
All that wine
The second bottle may have been a little much

His fingers pinch an invisible inch

Bring my lips to his finger
Suck it
He smiles
Eyes closed
He slurs

You're too much
Too much fun

He laughs slow and dumb

Kind of weird

Though
You're not like how I thought you'd be
You're different to how you sounded online

I want him to stop talking
Try to take the glass out of his hands
He says

Hang on, hang on

Downs it

Hands it to me empty
I put it down on the table
He's about to tell me to put it on the coaster but I take his
lip with my teeth
Straddle him
Won't kiss me back
Says

Wait

Tongue in his mouth
Lick his pearly whites
Grind my hips
Feel his hard-on
Kiss his neck
Unbutton his shirt

He grabs my hands
Says

No, no

He doesn't mean it
No grip in his hands
Giggles like a girl

What are you doing?

Does it feel good?
Do you like my lips?
Shall I suck your dick?

He giggles again

You're making me blush

He lifts my head

Let's just talk

But I want to fuck

No, no, we shouldn't, I'm too drunk
Why are you not drunk?
I don't know what drunk means

Rise up on my knees
Tower over him
Run my hands through his hair
His eyes are closing
He sinks
Shrinks
Into the sofa
Unbutton his trousers
Unzip
Rip
Grip
Stiff
Skin tightens
Thick and firm
Push my knickers to one side and
Feel him inside
Rise
Roll my hips forward
Rock back
He mumbles
He groans
Rolling towards my pleasure
I push
Strap of my dress falls off my shoulder
Tip of my nipple in line with his lips
Whisper slips from his mouth
no

Falls deafly on the
Roar
Of my
Orgasm
Eyes open
Whirling in his head

Get off me
Get OFF!

Shaking
Shouting
Puts his hands on my chest to push me away but his hot
clammy hands on my breasts make me come harder
Grips me under the arms
Guttural shriek pierces the heat
Not from him
From me
From my wet mouth
Blood where I bit the inside of my cheek
Agony splits me open
From where his hand is holding me up
Underarm
I look down at his hand
Clamp his wrist away
Fingers glistening with decay
Lump
Thumping

Throbbing
Purulent
Dripping
On my dress
On his sofa
Holds his hand up to the light to see
He snarls

What the fuck?
WHAT THE FUCK IS THAT?

Overcome with disgust
Spittle on his lips
Face is dark
Mine is darker

Flaws find their way
Bring pain
But the tumour is not mine
It swells up like a bee sting

He is screaming beneath me
His legs twitch and twist
Tries to throw me from his lap
I'm not going anywhere
Thighs thickly rope around him
Press my face against his
He has hot tears

Hands trapped by the weight of me
Green silk of my dress gropes him

Get off me!
Get off me, you psycho bitch!
Freak!
I'm going to be sick!
Get OFF!

I lean backwards
Feel my muscles tighten
Veins rise to the surface clotting with life
Tumour bulges
Taking breaths
By itself
He shifts beneath me
Hands freed
Snatches my throat
Catches my laugh
Strength isn't real
Limp fingers
His look is horror. Confusion. Anger.
Surely he'd be on top
I'd be underneath
Surely he'd be coaxing and I would come around
Never in his life lose control
Never in his life take his eye off the ball
Can't squeeze the life out of me

Hands won't obey
Will his fingers leave marks
Loosen his grip
Lose grip
Can't take his glazing eyes off the growth
Still growing
Engorged
He is going green
Rasping
Dumbly struggling
Doesn't see me reach for the ashtray
Doesn't see me swing it
Bring it down on his head
Like a brick
Bash his brains in
Skull cracks
Blood rains
Smash again
Shut my eyes to shield from the splatter
Concrete clatters to the floor
Stand up
Step back
Survey
Body folding
If it wasn't for the blood, rolling rivers of rubies
Shards of bone, sparkling, startlingly white
He might be sleeping

I stand here crying
Darkness is dying
Tumour is gorging on my time
Hands come together
Clasped

Prayer

Clap.

Lights go out.

devil had been long caged

So much salt dissolved in the water.

I float.

Heat, steam, scent of lavender knocks me out.

I lie back, close my eyes and drift. My arms curl under my body and feel the inches between my bones and the bathtub. The space has increased. I am wasting. My mind is a vacuum, blissfully black and empty, but my body remembers. Ache in my arm from holding something heavy, belly stretched and bloated from a phantom meal. Head underwater hearing pipes moan their burden of being always open. Mice. Bigger than that, rats tapping, little pink feet scrabbling up the walls. Human footsteps, a door opening, a voice, a face hovering above the water.

Rosy?

He looks pissed off.

I suck the air as I emerge, slick my hair back off my face and open my eyes.

Yeah?

What are you doing?

I'm having a bath, Charlie, what does it look like?

I lean back and rest my head on the rim.

Where have you been? he says.

I could ask you the same thing, I say, smiling sweetly.

I've been at work! It's been really busy and I've been worrying about you all night.

Has something happened?

Some guy has been bludgeoned to death.

I stifle a yawn.

I'm sorry you had a bad shift, I say. I reach for his hand, press my palm to his, extend my fingers and slip them between his. He softens, sits on the side of the bath.

It wasn't bad, he says, just busy. And this poor guy, properly coshed. Turns out he's a famous designer, or at least he was, or at least he was going to be. He was found in his house this morning, the police aren't saying who he was found by but the fact they won't tell us makes us think it was someone *really* famous. His house is in a mews in Notting Hill. Worth a fortune.

I might have to go back in to cover tonight, we're short-staffed again. If we don't get this sort of story right, we could get sued.

He dips his fingers into the water.

Jesus!

Pulls them back.

It's boiling! How can you lie in that!

It's soothing, I say.

He leans in and kisses me on my forehead.

Of course, he says, I'm sorry.

Do you know what else would soothe me, I say, taking his fingers, running them over my lips, kissing them softly, easing his hand slowly into the water, placing it on my breast, bringing it slowly down over my stomach.

Rosy... he says.

I touch his fingers lightly to my labia. I want him to touch me.

What are you doing? Come on, stop...

He tries to move his hand away but I hold it there.

I can't do that, he says.

Why not?

I just can't, you're ill, it doesn't feel right, he says.

I'm not ill, I say.

I don't want to do this now, he says, just have your bath, you'll feel better after.

He tries to stand up, but I pull him back to me, he slips, nearly falls into the water, sleeves soaking wet.

Seriously, what are you doing? You're acting so strangely. It's not funny, it's not a game, you're ill and you're not behaving rationally.

Rationally? I'm not behaving rationally?

My blood is boiling. It's all too red, too hot. I want to scream like a kettle.

He's standing in the doorway. He waits.

I tell him I'm not ill, you can't call what I am ill: illness is easy, illness is fixed with sleep and antibiotics and time. What I am is *ending*, nothing fixes it, nothing changes it, time is only spent, so please, please, let's not waste any more. Can't we just try to be together, like we used to?

He looks back at me. I am kneeling in the water, my arms are open wide, I'm reaching out to him. He looks at my face, he sees the tumour, he turns away and says not like this.

turn sick and white with the desire to kill him

What was I thinking?

I wasn't thinking. I was walking, I let my legs carry me, my last legs, let them lead me to where they wanted to go, where they last stood steadily, where they never thought they would be cut down. Hacked, untidily, with the bluntest axe.

Rosy, sit down.

Clinging to the last untethered tendon.

Please, have a seat.

Hands hover over my shoulders. I could thrash against him, I could resist, but his face tells me he's already very concerned about me, worried for me, he's got a panic button under his desk and he's not afraid to press it, or worse, he'll call Charlie to come and collect me.

I surrender.

I sit.

Silent sigh of relief. He sits behind his desk, hands where I can see them, showing me if I behave reasonably, so will he.

I'm not being unreasonable. I just want to work.

Please, Mr Jones. I just want to see the children again. Just for a couple of hours to begin with, then as I get better, I could stay longer until I'm up to full days again. Jess is brilliant, I know she'll be willing to support me.

Jess is brilliant, he says. She's teaching your class full-time now.

But she's not qualified.

You're right, she isn't, but you've taught her wonderfully, she knows what she's doing, she knows the children and they respond very well to her. For now, she's doing a good job until we can find proper cover.

But you won't need any cover if I come back, I say. My hands are claws, open, grasping.

Rosy, you can't come back, he says, looking down at his desk.

Regret. He is upset. I can feel it. It softens me. I slump.

You know that we miss you, the children miss you, you know that, but if you're being honest with yourself right now, do you think you can come back here and work, even just a few hours a day? Are you really well enough, strong enough?

Should I tell him what he wants to hear?

Should I throw a book at him?

You need to take care of yourself. Charlie said you're not receiving any more treatment. Shouldn't you be at home, resting? We're all very worried about you. I'm going to phone him, in fact, he can come and take you home.

Pity. Patronising.

The speed with which I scrape the chair back and stand startles him.

Thanks

For

Nothing.

I throw open the door and storm down the corridor, filling the space with my fury. I drag my brittle nails along the walls, tearing through the pictures and displays outside the classrooms. Bitterness spills out of my eyes, the world is dissolving around me. Where will I go now? What will I do?

Something small and squelchy slaps into my shins, it squeals when I step on it, screams as I leave it in a heap.

Jess bursts from behind a classroom door.

Oliver! Are you OK?

She runs to the crying child.

I walk on.

Mrs Winter! Rosy! Come back! she calls after me. Buzz of bodies, tiny shoes tapping on the tiles, running to their friend. Little voices.

Oh no!

Ollie!

Miss! Miss! He's fallen over!

Miss! Miss! He's bleeeeeding!

Rosy. Are you seriously just going to ignore and leave? I saw what you did.

She's coming after me. Half running, half walking, she taps my shoulder. She wishes she hadn't when I spin around.

Whiteness floods her face like spilt milk, she shudders, tries to speak with her dry mouth, can't. Her eyes are black with doom. She sees death.

plentiful springs of distress

Incredible how quickly it breaks down. I'm amazed and disgusted at the same time. I can't see it and that's a blessing but I can feel it. Oh, I can feel it. Top layer of skin sheared off, like I've been unzipped, someone pouring lemon juice on the world's biggest paper cut forever.

Sharon explains to me why superficial things sting the most. She tells me whilst I'm lying on my side, naked from the waist down, buttocks spread, Charlie standing next to her watching how she applies the layer of sticky barrier paste to the lesions around my anus. I'm not really listening to her, I'm watching my dignity sail out of the window. Sharon is gentle and kind, she's in my home, she has made sure I'm comfortable, she is showing my husband how to do this for me because I can't do it myself, and I can't bear the thought of strangers doing this for me twice a day.

Charlie listens intently. He trusts Sharon in her navy-blue uniform, green lanyard tucked into her top pocket and plastic apron for infection-control purposes. And he likes her because she doesn't treat him like an idiot. She uses the right amount of medical language, terms he'll have heard Dr Carson using and will have looked up on his phone in waiting rooms. She can tell when he doesn't understand something she has said because he will nod and his hand will hover near his pocket. When this happens, she'll say it again and make out like she's having to explain to me and she knows that I won't mind, it doesn't matter because everything at this point is for Charlie's benefit and nothing much matters to me any more.

You see? Just a very thin layer and only on the broken bits of skin. And then you apply the Vaseline over the top, and you want it to be a very thick layer so that it doesn't stick to the pad.

I can't see Charlie's face, but I can picture it. Serious, critical, unfazed. The face he made when Joe and Sally brought over a rabbit to be jointed and cooked. How long for? The cooking time?

How long? How long until it heals? he asks.

It's difficult to say, says Sharon. The skin isn't really the issue, it's the moisture. When the diarrhoea settles, and the stools become more formed then there won't be as much moisture on the skin and skin heals well when nutrition is optimised.

She touches my shoulder and leans over to look me in the eyes.

So, Rosy, that means you have to try and eat, she says, smiling.

I am trying, I say. But the more I try, the worse the diarrhoea gets.

We're in a vicious cycle, says Charlie.

Sharon nods understandingly.

Charlie goes out of the bedroom to wash his hands. Sharon helps me to turn on my other side. She sits on the bed next to me.

How are you feeling? she asks.

I say it once. This is the only time. I whisper it to her so Charlie doesn't hear. He may see it, he may know it, but he will never hear me say it.

I'm in so much pain.

She takes my hand in both of hers and begins to gently massage the thin tissue of my fingers, around the joints. Her brown hands are soft and feel like satin to my skin, so long untouched. She turns my hand over and kneads the palm. I stretch out my fingers and say: do you see?

What am I looking at? Besides your skin and bones.

I hold her index finger with my other hand and run it along the lines.

Look, faint life line, strong fate line.

She raises her eyebrows, continuing to massage my hand and reaching up to the measly meat of my arm.

Rosy, I can't help you unless you're open with me. When I came last week you told me the anti-inflammatory tablets were enough. Are you taking them?

Yes.

But you're not eating?

I'm trying. I grit my teeth.

I think we need to talk to Dr Carson about something stronger. We talked about the syringe driver before, didn't we, when you were in hospital last time. It's the little intravenous pump we can set up for you here.

But I don't have my line any more, I say.

That's OK, this time we can put it subcutaneously, so that will be a really small, really fine needle going into your thigh or tummy and it sits just under the skin. We can give you something stronger that way. What do you think?

I nod.

OK. I'll get Dr Carson to do the prescription. I can come back this evening and get you set up. Sound good?

The word thanks wobbles out. I don't want to start crying.

She leaves the barrier paste and the biggest tub of Vaseline I've ever seen in the plastic box by the side of the bed. Stack of nappies. My supplies. Like a fucking baby.

Charlie lets me sleep.

i have brought on myself
a punishment

Incredible how quickly it heals, says Charlie.

Sharon is grinning. She hugs me.

Look at you! Up and out of bed. Amazing.

I'm smiling. I've got the syringe driver in a little bag on my shoulder. It feels good to be up and about.

Sharon and I sit down on the sofa.

Now, she says. How is the pain?

Better, I say, smiling.

And the diarrhoea?

Better, I say, smiling.

Charlie says, yep, and her bottom is much less red and broken. Should I carry on with the paste stuff?

Mind if I have a look? says Sharon.

OK.

We go into the bedroom. I pull my knickers down and lie on the bed. Gloved fingers prod.

Great, it really is much better, I'm pleased, says Sharon. We can stop the paste now but let's use a barrier-film spray, just to keep your skin protected. And that will be much better for you, Rosy, you can do it yourself, twice a day.

I can see a sliver of Charlie's reflection in the mirror. He looks disappointed.

Sharon sprays me with something cold, and then it soothes. I pull my knickers up and roll onto my back.

Oh. Rosy. What's going on here?

Sharon looks down at my belly. I look too. I can just see the tips of my toes over the top of the bulbousness. She takes her gloves off and rubs her hands with alcohol gel. A little bit sticky, a little bit damp, her hands press my belly.

I could pop you like a balloon!

That's not... not... the tumour... is it? It's not, like, another one? asks Charlie. He reaches for my hand.

No. I'm constipated. I haven't been since I've had the syringe driver.

Ah, yes, that *is* one of the side effects, says Sharon.

But my skin is healed and I'm not in any pain, I say. So, it's the lesser of evils.

Sharon shakes her head.

You're going to get pretty uncomfortable pretty quickly. I'm surprised you're not already, you're very distended. I'll ask Dr Carson to prescribe some laxatives.

When Sharon has left, I stand cradling my belly in the mirror. I could be pregnant. My back curves. I have a glow. It's not a healthy glow, not a life-giving glow, but a sickly sheen, ghastly glitter around my eyes. Charlie comes in, catches me cooing over my unbirthed excrement.

What are you doing?

Nothing.

Are you pretending you're pregnant?

So what if I am?

Rosy. Don't. Just rest.

Why didn't we have a baby?

He sucks all the air out of the room through his nose. He paces. I turn to him, hands on my belly.

Don't do that, he says.

I step towards him, rubbing my roundness.

Don't.

He has no answer for me.

I have no answer for him.

We stand and look at each other until I need to sit down. Days of rock-hard stool stretch my sphincter; the pain is sharp and I want to cry.

leave her screaming

Please can you pass me the adhesive remover? It's that little wipe there, in the silver and green packet. Can you open it for me? Just rip the top of the packet, that's it. Thanks.

Sally hands it to me. She looks worried.

What? I say, peeling back a corner of the dressing. I use the wipe to ease off the rest.

Should you be doing this on your own? she says.

Well, who else is going to do it? I laugh.

Isn't there a nurse who comes to see you? Shouldn't you leave it for her?

Sharon? Yeah, I miss Sharon. She was lovely. All of the nurses were lovely. But no one comes now, no one has been for ages.

She swivels on the toilet to face the wall, she doesn't want to see it. Don't blame her.

Really? Shouldn't they be checking on you?

Checking I'm still alive, you mean?

I grit my teeth. I clean it with gauze and saline and it stings like a bitch. The gauze comes away stained with purulent, yellow goo. I place the silicone layer, then the charcoal layer, then the absorbent layer, then the dressing. I'm quick at it now, a dab hand, my mother would be proud.

Surely someone should be coming to see your wound to check it's healing?

I tap her on the shoulder. She turns to me. With pride, I lift my arm to show her the clean dressing.

See? It's easy. I don't need anyone to come and do it for me. And it's not a wound. It's not healing. It's not going to heal.

Can we go into the living room? It's hot in here, she says.

Sure, let me just clean these bits up.

I seal the dirty dressing and used gauze into the little orange plastic bin bag. Sally washes her hands in the sink, she looks at her face in the mirror.

God, I look haggard, she says. Look at these bags under my eyes! I'll have to call the bin men round to collect them! Haha!

I laugh, stand close behind her, rest my chin on her shoulder.

Thank you for being here, I say.

Of course, she says. Where else would I be?

I don't know, in the gang with everyone else who can't bear to be around me, I say.

Come on, you know it's difficult for Charlie, he doesn't cope well when he's not in control, she says, drying her hands. She opens the medicine cupboard. Got anything good in here?

Difficult for Charlie, I say flatly.

Rosy, come on, you know what I mean. He's worried sick, he desperately doesn't want to lose you.

But I'm lost already.

Mirrored glass swings slowly shut. Our sad reflections see each other. Her sad reflection sees something else. Her eyes moisten and widen like spilt oil, her jaw hangs. Something black and wet drips down my leg, splattering the white tiles. Oh. At first, I think it is coming from the tumour, but the dressing is clean, I touch it, it is dry.

Blackness spreads, wetness soaking through my top, matting my hair, sodden fingers crawling up my back, sprawling into thick sludge, pouring to the floor like a waterfall. She takes shape. Rising. Taller than us. Bulging head and no face. Slit for lips stretching open to a wide black hole.

Sally is screaming she backs towards the door cracks her elbow on the doorframe trying to reach the handle throws the door open and runs try to run after her but I am grabbed grasped hold onto the doorframe with desperate fingers digging into the wood splintering as I am dragged backwards try to scream for Sally but as my mouth opens her mouth opens and I am swallowed whole.

recall me to myself

I search for her. In pools of light, raindrops, reflections. I glance in mirrors, look for a long time in windows. I sit in pitch-dark. I sit in pitch-dark and light candles. Hover over a drawn bath. Peer into the creases of skin under my breasts, between my legs. I ask Charlie if he's seen her but he says he doesn't know who I mean and I believe him. He never really knew her. Not sure I did either.

But I did feel hunger that wasn't in my belly
Hands touching hips
Licking someone else's lips
Hearing a fast-beating heart, feeling my own slow pulse
Pulling the bedsheet up over my eyes, only to open them outside, blinking in the bright world.

I call out for her. I know she would answer me if she could.

We are creatures eaten up and emptied by fever.

time awfully fails me

Last few mornings Charlie has been waking me when the sun rises. He washes my face with a wet soapy flannel. He brushes the last of my hair. He buttons me into clean cotton pyjamas. I can walk a little still, but when he scoops me up into his arms and my nose nuzzles against his neck, I don't want to let go.

He lowers me gently into the wicker chair on the balcony and tucks a blanket over my knees. Sits and reads to me for an hour before he goes to work. I wave to him from the balcony, he blows me a kiss with one hand and reaches into his pocket for his phone with the other. I watch him disappear down the road. He tries not to use his phone around me. My phone is switched off, in a drawer somewhere. I asked him to get rid of it but he wouldn't. For emergencies, he said. But there won't be any. All arrangements have been made. When it happens it will be quiet and slow and I will do my best to be alone.

i shall sit shuddering and weeping in my chair

Last morning. I let him wake me and wash me, but I don't want to sit out on the balcony today. He lies down next to me on the bed and holds me. We don't talk about anything in particular. We don't understand and we don't agree, but we do forgive.

He is reluctant to leave me. He strokes my arm, kisses my neck. I close my eyes and it feels like it used to. I think he knows this will be the last time. He says he could stay; says he doesn't care about work any more. I touch his stubbled cheek and tell him to go, tell him to carry on, tell him I'll be here when he gets home. That's when our eyes fill, and we kiss long and lasting.

He closes the door. I wait for his descending steps. Another door closing. I listen. When I'm sure he's gone I pull back the quilt, swing my legs out of bed and sit at the edge, letting the colours and the blood settle. I go to the wardrobe and rummage around at the back for the box. I slip off the thick cardboard lid and take out the dresses. Run my fingers through the silks, spread them out on the bed. They are gleaming amber and emerald jewels in the morning light. The green one, my favourite, is splattered with dried blood. Try to brush it off but the droplets are thick and rusty, breaking and flaking, little fragments, garnet glitter.

Unbutton my pyjamas. Fingers move slowly, conscious of spending energy. I step into the dress. Straps hang onto my shoulders for dear life as the silk drowns me. I look at myself in the mirror. No curves to caress, no flesh to brush. I am stick-like, a hairpin. And a bulge, breathing on its own, suckling like a plump baby, draining me. Pale as paper, lips a sliver, drawn, baring my useless teeth. I wrap my head in the orange silk slip. The effort of raising my arms is too much. I sit, I fight the urge to lie back down. If I lie down, I won't get back up again. I watch my chest stutter in the mirror. Ribcage opening to release the last of my breaths.

Sun moves slowly across the sky. I watch it, warming in the rich rays when they reach me. Like a lizard on a rock, I steal enough energy to stand again and then I move quickly.

Lightheaded, light as air, feet bare, bones of a bird, tapping, snapping like twigs on the floor and then the concrete, make it to the balcony, grip the railings, lean over the edge to wave goodbye to the world. Trees awaken in the wind, they dance for me, they wave. I hear them whisper *Rosy* in the rustling of their copper leaves.

Whisper again, *Rosy, Rosy, Rosy*. Feel the breeze on my cheek and then in my ear there is the tip of a tongue the tip of a tongue there are fingers on my neck on my back stroking my spine the fingers spell her name on my shoulder blades and then the blade of her voice cuts through sharply shrieking shattering the glass doors behind me I turn into her ferocity she is a thousand pieces many many multiplying she is flying towards me her arms are stretched she rips out of flesh out of flesh and bones flung and flailing. She feels for me, feels me. Thought she was going to throw me, but her fingers feel me tenderly. I can barely take her all in with my failing eyes, she is gushing energy, she is a flowing fountain of silver and gold, she is like nothing I have ever seen before but I have seen her. I know her. Her cheek is against mine, her hands hold mine. She lifts me up and we spin. Listen. Sounds of joy. Fingers entwined, twirling for the last time. A last look at her face, a last look at mine and I go dancing over the edge.